She knew she'd been dreaming of this through ever love story on TV, through every video she rented, through every car she painted at the body shop, long before she'd ever known Regina. She'd always wanted to be the one kissing the girl. Nothing else would have felt right to her.

Regina was unbuttoning her blouse.

Andy looked down the street.

"It's the middle of the night, Andy. No one who's out this late is up to any better than we are."

"This wasn't how I thought we'd spend our honeymoon."

"Honeymoon? Get real, Andy Blaine. I didn't marry you, I ran away with you."

Andy wanted those breasts in her hands right now more than she'd ever wanted anything in her life. The car wasn't under a street lamp, so maybe it was safe. She moved close to hot, perfumey Regina and pulled the two cups together where they hooked in front. Globular, rose-tipped, Regina's breasts spilled out onto her hands. There wasn't a thing smoother under the sky . . .

Critics say about Lee Lynch:

"Every once in a while you find an author who seems to produce book after book which you *know* you will enjoy. . . . . *The Swashbuckler* is a wonderful story of an earlier time, with all the excitement and danger it produced. This will be a welcome addition to all those bookshelves of lesbian novels."

— *Out!*

"Like all of Lee Lynch's books and stories, *Dusty's Queen of Hearts Diner* is rich with characterization and loving, detailed descriptions. The lesbians and gay men are shown to be proud, vulnerable, strong, passionate, independent, possessive, righteous — and sometimes dead wrong . . ."

— *Gay Community News*

"*Toothpick House* is a beautifully written novel that realistically depicts the varied contemporary Lesbian and feminist lifestyles. Simply put, it is the love story of the working class dyke . . ."

— *Gaze*

"Lee Lynch offers us a clever detective story told from the perspective of a tiger cat named Sue in this tale, *Sue Slate: Private Eye*. If you are an animal lover, curl up with your favorite pet and enjoy Lee Lynch's witty work. If not, reading *Sue Slate* may make you an instant cat fan."

— *Lambda Rising Book Report*

"You don't have to be a 'cat person' to enjoy *Sue Slate*. Lynch, the popular author of *Old Dyke Tales, The Amazon Trail* and *Dusty's Queen of Hearts Diner*, among others, has created another fine work . . ."

— *Bay Area Reporter*

That Old Studebaker

BY
LEE LYNCH

The Naiad Press, Inc.
1991

Printed in the United States of America on acid-free paper
First Edition

Edited by Christine Cassidy and Katherine V. Forrest
Cover design by Pat Tong and Bonnie Liss
    (Phoenix Graphics)
Typeset by Sandi Stancil

Library of Congress Cataloging-in-Publication Data

Lynch, Lee, 1945—
    That old Studebaker / by Lee Lynch.
        p.   cm.
    ISBN 0-941483-82-7 : $9.95
    I. Title.
PS3562.Y426T47   1991
813'.54--dc20   90-21905
                                                                      CIP

FOR AKIA WOODS

Thank you for the fullness of my life with you.

What ever happened to the gypsy in me,
To the free lifed woman that I thought I
   would be?
Now she's putting down roots with a family
   and a home
And the love she's always longed to call her
   own.

from the song "Full Circle" by Akia Woods

Acknowledgments

Many people have helped me in various ways to write this book over a period of seven years. Among them are: Akia Woods, Katherine Forrest, Carol Seajay, Tee Corinne, Debbie Pascale, Lynn Johnson, The Listen and Be Kind Lesbian and Gay Writers' Group, the Southern Oregon Women's Writers' Group, Niman, Susan Koppleman, and Mayumi Tsutakawa. Thank you all.

Thanks to Judy Grahn for permission to use lines from "Confrontations With the Devil in the Form of Love" (p. 148) in her book *The Work of a Common Woman*, Crossing Press, 1978.

The ritual in Chapter Sixteen is based on one found in Z. Budapest's *The Holy Book of Women's Mysteries*.

Love came along and saved
no one
Love came along, went broke
got busted, was run out of
town and desperately needs —
something. Don't tell her it's Love.

Judy Grahn
from "Confrontations With the Devil
in the Form of Love"

CHAPTER ONE

Andy was redheaded and scowled a lot. She was probably the most unsociable person in the universe. She'd as soon spit as look at you and sometimes she did spit, if a man made remarks at her.

Almost the only thing Andy loved in the world was that old Studebaker her father thought he had run into the ground. He sold it to her for fifteen dollars without a second thought. Fixing cars came naturally to her and she'd been working in her dad's garage since she was old enough to see under a hood. She got the Studebaker running good. Then she got herself a job over at Lake Auto Wash to pay for used parts and gas.

One thing always leads to another. Shining up those fancy cars at work made Andy realize how dull and unloved the body of her Studebaker looked, so she washed and polished it regularly and began to replace the chrome bit by bit. The boss from BB's Bump and Paint Parlor, who sometimes brought them jobs to do, noticed Andy's brilliantly polished Studebaker and offered her a painting job which would give her more hours. When she hesitated, hating to make yet another change in her life, he told her she could have a free coat of black paint for her car, and she followed him to his shop.

Andy still didn't talk to anybody, but one day when she'd been at the body shop a couple of weeks she met this woman. She was the prettiest woman Andy ever saw, maybe because she'd never been interested enough to look before. The woman was admiring her Studebaker.

This pretty woman, whose name was Regina, was girlfriend to one of the other painters, named Roy. He had an old Chevy which he'd souped up for racing. It was a real impressive car, Andy thought, and much faster than the Studebaker. She wondered which car the pretty woman liked better. Not that she cared.

Regina began hanging around the painting shop a lot, leaning up against the cars. Roy's mostly, but sometimes Andy's.

Besides the Studebaker, the only other thing in the world Andy loved was country/western music. She'd fixed up the Studebaker with a working radio and played it real loud on long rides in the country.

2

One reason the body shop, even though it stank, was a better place to work than the car wash, was because the guys always played the radio on the country/western station from Concord and they played it real loud.

Andy had never danced, but sometimes, especially when she caught sight of Regina leaning against the Studebaker, she found herself doing funny little steps and hops to the good songs.

While all these new things were going on in Andy's life — the Studebaker, the pretty woman, her job — Roy and the boys were always talking about drag racing. Andy became so fascinated by it, she listened more and more closely to their talk. Since she couldn't seem to ask questions, or for help, she began to study the car magazines on the drugstore shelf. She'd stay there reading them so long the counter clerks would remind her she wasn't at a library and kick her out.

Then she'd go straight home to tinker with the Studebaker, making it roar in ways she thought sounded like Roy's car. When she left the painting shop nowadays she'd roar away, hoping Regina would be impressed.

One day as Andy was about to rev up her engine, Regina came over and began to talk, hanging in the car window chewing gum, just like she did with Roy. Andy got one whiff of her perfume, her Marlboro breath, her Juicy Fruit gum, all exaggerated by hot woman sweat, and thought her heart would pump right out of her mouth.

Regina talked about this and that, seeming to understand Andy wouldn't give her much in the way of answers. After a while Regina led her conversation around to dancing.

"I see you like to dance some."

"Who, me?"

"Well, you have good rhythm."

Andy couldn't very well say "Who, me?" again, so she blushed into the roots of her red hair.

"You mean you don't know how to dance?" Regina asked.

Andy shook her head no, ashamed.

"Want me to teach you?"

And so they began to meet in the evenings, at Regina's house, where they would dance to Michael Jackson one record, Madonna the next, until Roy revved his engine outside and Regina had to go.

Every evening it got a little harder to let Regina go, so to prevent that, Andy found herself talking. She would talk a blue streak until she was too embarrassed to go on. She never guessed she had so much to say to one person before.

One night there was something in the air. Andy wondered, was this what they called spring fever? She got to Regina's in an excited state after eating hardly any dinner at all, but taking two showers. Regina, too, seemed different. She kept forgetting to teach Andy new steps so they ended up just dancing to a lot of old slow songs. Andy realized it had been weeks since Regina had last predicted she would be a fine dancer some day and would catch herself a boyfriend.

On this night Roy revved so long Andy was scared he'd run out of gas. Still they danced and danced and danced. Andy weaving words she didn't know she had in and out of their rhythm together, as if to make a chain to bind Regina to her. She'd never guessed she'd fall in love with a girl, but at least she finally knew why she'd always been so different from everyone else.

All at once Regina pushed Andy away and ran outside. Sighing, Andy tucked in her good shirt and got ready to leave. But Regina rushed back in, all smiles.

"I told him I got the curse," she explained.

Andy squinted her eyes to understand, then blushed when she figured out what the curse was, then heard Roy roar away, and she smiled too.

Regina went to Andy and they danced long into the night, until they were so tired they lay down together and even then they didn't really stop dancing. Andy felt this creeping warmth that made her shake, made her sweat, made her, wondrously, cry as she touched the soft places on Regina's body and watched the woman move in ways that were like dancing she hadn't learned to do yet.

After that, Regina began to lean on Andy's Studebaker at the body shop a whole lot more than she leaned on Roy's Chevy. She didn't see much of Roy evenings anymore either.

Roy started looking at the two of them strangely. One night, like some crazy terrorist, he barged into the room where Regina and Andy did their dancing, and he began to shout, to call them names. Then he said, "You want a woman?" to Andy. "You prove you're man enough first. I'll meet you on Rollercoaster Road tonight at eleven and race you for the woman. If you don't show or if you lose, either one, I get her. Looks like I just got to show her who's the real man around here."

When he slammed out of the room Regina cried, sobbing about how it would be if she gave up Roy for a woman.

Andy hadn't said a word the whole time Roy was there, but she rose to the challenge now, full of words like, "I'll beat the pants off that boy." She spent the rest of the evening in her Studebaker, waiting for the old church clock to strike half past ten. Secretly, she was quaking. Of course she couldn't win. She hadn't known enough about cars to make her Studebaker as fast as Roy's Chevy. But maybe, with a little luck . . . She looked toward the heavens. The stars were twinkling up there like they did in her head when Regina did those things to her that felt so good.

She could hear Regina still crying in the room where they danced, probably wondering what to do. When it was time to go, Regina ran to the Studebaker, tissues wadded in her hand, and got in. She looked miserable.

"I don't want to lose you, Andy, but I'm too scared to choose you."

"Maybe the race is the best way to decide," Andy said.

When they got to Rollercoaster Road it looked like all of Weirs Beach had heard about this race between the man and the woman who thought she was a man. But out of all those kids, Andy didn't have one damn person rooting for her. At least now she knew what made her so unsociable. She didn't have anything to say to those normal people at all.

She dropped Regina at the end of the strip and came back to the start line.

The kids lined the route, making ugly threats at Andy. She spit out the window into the wild flowers at the side of the road, then stroked that old Studebaker, admitting to herself and the car it would do fine now on long distances, the shape she'd got it in, but it wasn't cut out for racing. Maybe she just ought to ride out of town and clear across the country before she made a fool of herself. But to leave Regina behind without even trying?

Roy revved. Andy answered. "I'm counting on you," she told the Studebaker. The stars were still twinkling through the windshield, like they knew a secret and were teasing her.

Next thing she knew the starter signaled, Roy was off, and she was on his tail, trying the best she could to keep up with him.

She couldn't. Not only that, but she felt so bad for the old Studebaker, whose V6 engine she'd so lovingly restored, that she slowed down, letting Roy's new V8 win by a whole lot more than he should have, rather than hurt her car.

When she saw Regina at the finish line, she felt just like dying. Maybe she had saved the car she loved, maybe she couldn't have won the race anyway, but she'd lost the only woman she'd ever love.

Roy swaggered over to Regina. Andy could see him puckering his big lips for a victory kiss. He was the man, the natural winner, and maybe Regina would be better off with him anyway.

Looking at Regina one last time, Andy admired the body that made her shake and sweat so, the lips that brought stars into her head, the hands that made her dance even when she wasn't dancing. But as she looked she realized Regina wasn't giving Roy his kiss, wasn't even looking at him. Was she staring at the abomination of Andy, shocked she could have let such a loser ever touch her?

Andy started up the Studebaker as Regina began to run toward it. When it started as sweet as a brand new Cadillac Andy patted it quickly, certain it was thanking her for being kind during the race. As soon as Regina had slammed the door behind her, and settled as close to Andy as she could get, they were off.

That old Studebaker was anxious to prove that, yes, she was meant for a good long trip clear across the country.

Regina pleaded, "Let's drive all night, Andy. Let's never stop."

Andy allowed herself one last look in the rear view mirror at the astounded and diminishing Roy.

CHAPTER TWO

"Your eyes are the lightest blue I've ever seen on anyone," Regina said as she and Andy grinned at each other in the gas station in Burlington, Massachusetts. "Except maybe Mel Gibson."

They'd left Weirs Beach four hours ago. Andy had taken every back road on the map, trying to evade Roy. The night felt endless, they were still high with excitement, but they were going to stop at Boston.

They only had maybe fifty dollars between them.

"Don't worry, Andy. I've waitressed a dozen

restaurants on Lake Winnepesaukee. I can get work anywhere."

They decided to sleep in the car on a cobblestoned street in Back Bay.

"It's our first night together, Andy," said Regina as Andy squeezed into a parking space.

"I know," she said, chewing on her lower lip, a little nervous about really being with Regina forever. Now that she knew what she was, she knew she'd been dreaming of this through every love story on TV, through every video she rented, through every car she painted at the body shop, long before she'd ever known Regina. She'd always wanted to be the one kissing the girl. Nothing else would have felt right to her.

Regina was unbuttoning her own blouse.

Andy looked down the street.

"It's the middle of the night, Andy. No one who's out this late is up to any better than we are."

"This wasn't how I thought we'd spend our honeymoon."

"Honeymoon? Get real, Andy Blaine. I didn't marry you, I ran away with you."

Regina spread open her blouse and thrust her breasts toward Andy. "Help me with this bra, Andy. I know how much you like this part."

Andy wanted those breasts in her hands right now more than she'd ever wanted anything in her life. The car wasn't under a street lamp, so maybe it was safe. She moved close to hot, perfumey Regina and pulled the two cups together where they hooked in front. Globular, rose-tipped, Regina's breasts spilled out onto her hands. There wasn't a thing smoother under the sky. She played with them, watching their shape change under her hands.

"Use your mouth, Andy."

Regina liked when she sucked on them and she stopped feeling embarrassed by her noisy breathing in the silence of the car, the stillness of the city night as she heard Regina's breath come hard as her nipples.

She spread her hands around Regina's rib cage, slipped down to her waist, sent one hand under her slacks.

"Come *on,* lover," Regina insisted, unzipping herself, then stripping the pants down to her calves.

Andy was overcome by the wetness she found, the sweet-sharp Regina smell that filled the car. She pushed her fingers right into Regina, over the inside cliff, not even touching outside first. Regina moved on them, breathing, "Come on, come on," over and over into her ear. Andy thrust and thrust as far inside as she could go. She forgot this wasn't Regina's house, but a city street, she forgot that Regina thought this wasn't a marriage. It was marriage to her, and if the honeymoon took place in that old Studebaker instead of a bed, if the only souvenir would be a wet spot on the upholstery, then chalk it up to being different from all the regular honeymooners. She didn't care; she had Regina, Roy didn't.

"Oh, Andy, I'm drowning. I'm drowning."

It felt like Regina was trying to climb inside her she snuggled so close afterward. In a minute, though, she was reaching under Andy's shirt, rubbing her nipples hard, moving her hand to Andy's crotch and playing with that little nub of flesh that made Andy's breath short and made her think of long lazy summers on the lake, drifting in a rowboat in the heat of the day, then splashing into the warm water, feeling herself widen and widen down there, floating on the waves of passing motorboats and finally diving underwater as deep as she could hold her breath.

She broke the surface and gasped for air. Regina held her a while, then climbed into the back seat to sleep. Andy lay down and watched the sky lighten through the steering wheel, smelling their lovemaking, feeling their damp spots with her fingers, her limbs buttery, her heart full of love and her mind free of worry. There would be room for them here, in Boston.

Later that day it was easy to find a cheap room in South Boston. Regina did the talking; Andy's mouth filled with marbles when she spoke to anyone except Regina or her family. She called home collect at 5:00 to tell them where she was. Her mother cried a little at the suddenness, but how could Andy explain that she didn't have a choice?

"It can't be that bad, Smiley," employers said sarcastically when Andy, hands stuffed in her pockets, stuttered out a request for work in the next weeks. To make it worse, she only had the clothes she'd worn for the race. They looked her up and down, checking out her navy chinos and her Dad's garage shirt which had his name, Andrew, stitched above the pocket. When she put Andrea on the application they looked back up at her with sneers on their faces, and said they had no openings. She began to wonder if these men were all from places

12

like Weirs Beach. She didn't want to think about the possibility that Boston was just like home.

Regina landed a job at a downtown coffee shop before her clothes even got dirty. Then, in Regina's hours off, Andy washed her clothes for her in the bathroom down the hall from their room, inhaling perfume, knowing Regina wasn't wearing a stitch back there between the sheets. She could hear Tracy Chapman singing in someone else's room, taste the lasagna Regina had brought home in styrofoam trays from the coffee shop for dinner.

"It's so sweet, loving you," she told Regina under the bright Boston moon, strolling along the Charles River with all the murmuring people who'd been to hear the Boston Pops. And, "It's so sweet, being loved by you."

"You're always saying that," Regina said, slipping her bare arm through Andy's. "I'm not so sweet, to tell you the truth, but I love you for thinking I am. I'm going to call you my Sweet Andy from here on out."

"We're going to make ourselves a home, Regina Tonneau. I'll fix cars and you can be a lady of leisure like Princess Diana."

Back in their room she took soft, creamy-skinned Regina in her arms. Regina pulled her closer, breasts like hot velvet pillows.

Andy sighed, "I'll hold you all night long, every night, forever more." Then their joined heat rose up and swept them into kissing that always got Andy dizzy even before she reached Regina's breasts.

The waitress job in Boston lasted two weeks, until Andy found out what Regina had to do to the boss to keep it.

"It's better than starving," Regina said, her green-gold eyes challenging and pleading at the same time. "What with you wandering around Boston every day not getting any work." Regina broke down then and cried on Andy's shoulder.

When the crying was out of her system Regina started talking as tough as usual, almost bragging that the boss liked her. As if she was glad a man wanted her because it proved she wasn't really gay.

The smell of perfume gagged Andy. She didn't want to hit Regina, but she wanted to beat her fists against something to protest this betrayal. How dare anyone else touch her friend? How could Regina bring home some man's dirt? Being gay was the best thing that had ever happened to her. Why didn't Regina feel the same way?

She felt guilty. Hadn't she been slacking off on applying for jobs? How many times could she face these guys who looked at her like Roy had? After a while, just so she wasn't home doing nothing, she walked the city, looking for Help Wanted signs.

She'd rest in the cool, quiet art museums. During summer downpours people surged in, shaking their umbrellas, peeling off slippery-sounding nylon jackets and squeaking across the smooth polished floors, notepads sticking up from their canvas satchels, or arm-in-arm with middle-aged lovers.

The museum pictures took her out of herself, especially one show, with photographs of cars. Black Buicks in gas station lots in the 1930s, with the old round ESSO signs and people bunched around drinking Cokes out of a big ice chest. Convertible Cadillacs in front of palm trees and pink sunsets. Ornamented 1950s Chevies driven by kids in Los

Angeles. El Rancheros with guys in ducktails, arms around their girls. She wandered the Boston streets dreaming of the pictures she'd take. A portrait of the Studebaker, dark and gleaming, under a harvest moon.

Regina quit her job to keep Andy happy, but she stubbornly refused to look for another. She stayed at home instead, reading fat novels by Danielle Steele about glamorous women in big cities. Andy worked for a temporary agency, filling in as a cashier at self-service gas stations on the graveyard shift.

"You promised to support me, Sweet Andy," Regina cooed in bed one night under the magazine pictures she'd taken from the coffee shop. Regina had made a patchwork design at the head of their bed: Madonna, Prince, Janet Jackson, George Michael, Tracy Chapman and a scene from *Dirty Dancing*.

"Some day," she answered in a small voice. This wasn't what she'd expected; they were supposed to be partners and share everything. "I —" she started to say, but didn't want to get Regina mad. "We'll move on then. Maybe Boston isn't the place for us. Look at the restaurants back home."

Regina had bitten her ear and asked, "What makes you think that was any different?"

How could she be angry with Regina so close and her own passionate blood beating through her veins?

CHAPTER THREE

It was like leaving New Hampshire again. Andy felt swelled up with hope. Regina's eyes shone with excitement — and big ideas.

"Let's stop at the Americana Hotel in New York City," Regina said as Andy dodged the impatient and angry drivers thronging the road from Stamford into New York. Once they'd agreed to leave Boston Andy had wanted to skip all the coastal metropolitan areas. But Regina had never been to New York and wouldn't hear of bypassing it. Then, Regina said, they'd head west.

"It'd take all our gas money to stay at a big hotel. I thought we were just going to walk around a little and leave right away."

"You can't see New York City in one day, Andy."

"Then isn't there a Motel Six?"

"We have to stay someplace nice or it'll be just like anyplace else. This is special."

Regina wanted to be a heroine in one of her novels. Andy didn't reply.

"Then how about Howard Johnson's Motel? My cousin George stayed there for his honeymoon."

"I wouldn't even know how to find it. Besides, you said this isn't a honeymoon." They were on a highway that went down the east side of New York. She slowed until they could figure out what to do. Several cars passed them, horns blaring as Regina scraped old polish off her fingernails.

"We could drop in on my cousin Frenchy!" Regina exclaimed. "She lives in *Greenwich Village,*" she added in a conspiratorial whisper.

She remembered traveling to Manchester, the nearest city that would show daring movies, to see *Cruising* and Greenwich Village.

"You mean it runs in your family?" asked Andy.

"What?"

"Being, you know, like us." She was getting so nervous from the merging and passing cars and the sudden stops when traffic jammed up that she'd get off just about anywhere.

"It's not like it's a disease, Sweet Andy."

"Everybody treats me like it is. They just look at me and they can tell. Then they get so mean you'd think I was going to give it to them if I touched them."

17

"You are so naive! They're just scared they are too." Regina pulled a bottle of silver nail polish from her bag.

Andy tried to catch a glimpse of Regina's long thick dark hair which looked like it belonged on some rare and regal wild animal. In profile, Regina's nose hooked in that aggressive French way so many people in New Hampshire seemed to have. As they got older it made them look as gaunt and severe as Gramma, her Dad's ma, at the very end. Young, though, it was all pride and devil-may-care like the prow of a ship crossing the seas. It thrilled Andy, but Regina said it was too big.

Regina turned to her. In the twilight her eyes were mostly gold. She smelled of nail polish. "So are we going to Frenchy's?"

There was no way Andy could resist that wet-lipped look of supplication. They followed the highway downtown and plowed into the mad city. Andy had never been farther from home than Boston, and Boston had been nothing like these streams and rivers of traffic converging and parting without sense. She was terrified that one of the demonic cabs would wreck the Studebaker.

Regina rolled down her window and took a deep breath. "New York City!" she cried, wriggling on her seat. She turned a rock 'n roll station on loud.

Though she had to laugh at Regina's triumphant entry into the big city, complete with The Rolling Stones like a marching band on the radio, her laugh turned to a cough at the influx of bad air. "There's no place to stop," she complained over the roar of eight million people living at full speed.

It was true. All the parking spaces in Manhattan were taken and the rates advertised by the lots looked about like the price of a motel. She drove in circles through the sweltering city while Regina rummaged in her bag for an address book. Were those people lined up to buy crack right on the street like she'd seen on TV? Why was that woman walking five dogs at once? Small children shouted in a playground just like they would back home.

She almost got lost trying to get back to Regina's pay phone. Her cousin said to double-park outside her apartment building on Bank Street. It took Andy half an hour to fight her way through one way streets and horn-blowing natives.

"How could you want to live here?" she asked Regina.

"It's like going to the movies!" burst Regina. "It's like living in a big fat novel. It's like being born!" She tore her eyes away from two women striding past them. "No one would look twice at you here, Andy."

She followed the women with her eyes. "Think they're like us?"

Regina grinned. "Yes, and ten bucks says I'm right."

"Wouldn't that be nice. A place where nobody would care that I love you."

Frenchy strode out of a tall red brick apartment building. Andy could not believe how tiny she was. "Hell of a car," Frenchy told her, offering her hand.

Andy took it and gave her a big smile. After the drive there it was just the right thing to say. She couldn't feel shy at all around someone Frenchy's size.

Frenchy hopped in the back seat and leaned forward between them. "Do exactly like I say and we'll have you parked in no more than twenty minutes. Just so you know this won't take all night."

On West 12th, Regina cheered. "Only ten minutes, Andy! See, the city's not so bad."

"Is it going to be okay here?"

"You mean stolen?" Frenchy asked with a sideways grin. "As safe as anyplace in New York. This neighborhood has a citizen's patrol. Just be sure to get it out of here by eight a.m. tomorrow or the city will steal it."

All the way back to her apartment, she told them horror stories of car-towing ordeals. Then, over a home-cooked spaghetti dinner, Regina caught her up on the news of Frenchy's "country cousins."

"You know," Frenchy said, "I haven't been up there since I came out. I remember it as the kind of place where I'd stick out like a sore thumb."

"Andy was the closest thing to you in Weirs Beach," agreed Regina.

"How'd you get away with living there?"

Andy tried politely not to pick the black specks out of the thick red sauce where Frenchy had burned it. She shrugged. "I was just different. I didn't know I was anything bad. My folks, most of the kids I knew, I just didn't have anything to talk to them about."

"You were a gay kid, like me," said Frenchy, a look of pride in her eyes. "I didn't know what I was either, but me and Terry, my best friend, used to dress up in boys' clothes and have ourselves some adventures."

"Terry was a girl?" asked Andy.

"Under all those clothes she was all girl."

"I had a friend, a boy named Fletcher. We used to trade clothes. He'd wear my skirts and give me his pants. In the woods we'd make rooms out of leaves and pine needles. Then we'd play house, him the mother, me the father."

"And when you played with the other girls?"

She thought a minute. "I tried to get them to play cops or King of the Hill."

"Street hockey," bragged Frenchy.

She watched every move Frenchy made. Finally, someone else who felt like a loose end no one had ever bothered to ravel up. And she could tell by looking at her that it was okay with Frenchy to be gay.

When they went out Andy was amazed that this little fifty-year-old bird of a woman could navigate New York City. Frenchy threw her weight around as if she were somebody. And she knew all sorts of lesbians and faggots — whoops, she was supposed to call them gay men. At the neighborhood bar, she seemed to know everyone, the swishy guys and bulldaggery women, as well as the ones Andy couldn't tell were queer, like Regina.

"There must be hundreds of us here," Andy said, dazed.

"At least a few dozen," said Frenchy with a laugh. "Haven't you ever been to a gay bar before?"

Regina took her eyes off a woman in black leather long enough to say, "Been to one? There *isn't* one in that godforsaken town. I've heard of a place

21

in Centre Harbor, but it's for men. This is the place for me." She smiled into Andy's eyes and held her hand.

Regina's touch calmed Andy's stab of fear. What if Regina wanted to stay here with her cousin and the panhandling junkies and the bag people who wheeled their dirty rags and tatters in front of them in wobbly shopping carts?

Later that night, Regina sighed with contentment as they danced in the open-up bed. Regina insisted on leaving the shade up. Sometimes it seemed as if she were making love with the city, not with Andy.

"All those lights outside the window make me feel like half the world is watching us," whispered Andy.

"They are, Sweet Andy!" Regina whispered back, running to the window and standing fully naked against it, arms outflung, her graceful, slope-breasted body outlined by the city lights.

Andy wondered what it would be like to be Frenchy here with Regina, an old hand at the city and women. Or to be that black woman at the bar in the fedora, kind of drunk, laughing and dancing with a lot of women. Or the bartender, working every night in a place packed full of people like herself with the younger ones in pink spiked hair or nose rings sneaking peeks at her to see if she was interested. She could take her pick, be any of them. Regina was right, this was like being born!

The next day she called home and got her dad this time. He was still yakking about the rotten deal the judge had given Oliver North back in July. She could hear her ma nag him to let her talk. Andy assured her that she was eating well and asked her to tell Regina's family that they were just seeing America.

There wasn't a chance she'd say they'd eloped, even to her own folks. If she'd been a guy — but she wasn't, and she saw no reason to make her folks miserable. She loved them, but they just wouldn't understand. If her perky wiseass Gramma had been alive, she probably would have told Andy, "More power to you!" and bragged about her gay granddaughter all over town before anyone could criticize. She would have loved the race too, and Andy sort of winning. Sometimes she didn't see how they could all be in the same family, her and Gramma and her straight and narrow folks.

She and Regina stayed three days. Frenchy managed a grocery store on Sixth Avenue, but she worked weekends, so she was free to squire them around. They went to Coney Island, the Central Park Zoo, the Empire State Building, all the places Regina said she'd seen in movies or read about and dreamed of visiting. Andy's only request was Radio City Music Hall. She had an aunt who'd tried out for the Rockettes, but ended up teaching dance in Laconia.

Their last evening arrived none too soon for Andy. Regina had kept them out late every night, and when she finally went to sleep, Andy lay on the bed listening to the traffic which never stopped. She went over and over the lesbians she'd seen, wondering where she fit in. The big-city dykes her own age were very strange-looking, like the kind of rock stars Regina liked. Could she live like Frenchy or like them? Regina had gotten three more holes poked in her ears and had tried to teach her to dance to the crazy rock on the New York jukeboxes: AC/DC and Run-D.M.C.

"Don't you want to go to the bar tonight, Frenchy?" Regina asked.

"How about watching a video?" Frenchy suggested.

"On our last night?"

"Listen, Regina," Frenchy said. She'd gone back to work and sent them on the Staten Island Ferry that day and to the South Street Seaport. "City life isn't like your romantic novels, or even like this all the time," Frenchy explained. "There's a lot of drudgery to get the money to party. *I* can't go to the bar except on weekends. I can't afford it for one thing, even though I'm world champ when it comes to making one drink last. Or thought I was till Andy showed up. For another thing, I'm too tired. Don't get me wrong, I love this city, but it can wear you out."

Andy nodded. "This is gay paradise — if you can take it."

Frenchy lit a cigarette and looked intently at Regina. "Most days off I spend at the AIDS House, volunteering. We have gay people dying all around us. I'm not your Act Up type, but I go down to City Hall, rabble-rousing to make them keep the West Village just the way it is. Developers come in here all the time trying to make money with high-rises and tacky Times Square shops. Maybe that's the kind of sightseeing I should've taken you on, never mind the fun stuff. You know when I was last on the Ferry, which is one of my favorite things to do? Five years ago, when cousin Gerard came down. Life

24

in New York City is just like life in Weirs Beach, only there's a lot more people living it with you."

Andy had never seen Regina back off so fast. She stopped dropping hints that she needed a place to stay while she looked for a job.

"Oh, Andy," she'd finally said with a sigh as they lay in bed that night. "Am I ever going to be anything but a small-town tramp?"

"You're no tramp, Regina. Just like I'm no sophisticated Frenchy."

They left the next morning.

CHAPTER FOUR

Andy drove the Studebaker fast, to get far from the taint of big cities.

Regina became nicer. She kept crying about wanting to be able to settle down with Andy forever and being afraid she wasn't good enough to do that and how Andy was too good for her. Andy hadn't seen her do anything bad. Had Regina tried to dance in Frenchy's bed?

"You're so innocent, Andy. You never tell lies, you never went with men." Regina laughed then.

"And you always blush when I teach you something new in bed."

"I'll get a job and take care of you, Regina. Then you can stay home, out of harm's way."

"I wonder if I just am harm, and don't need to know the way."

Andy was sure that love would make Regina feel clean too. If she could just love her enough. She tried harder all the way to Ohio, but kept hearing Gramma's laugh: *Love and a nickel will get you a phone call.*

They stopped in Columbus, Ohio, and bought milk, bologna and a loaf of Wonderbread in an all-night grocery store. Andy was tired, but on top of the world again. Ohio felt like a mild, friendly place.

"Let's stop here a while and earn some money, Regina. I just know I can get a job in this kind of town."

"Isn't this where Laverne and Shirley lived? Remember that TV show? Columbus is not anyplace I ever dreamed of settling in."

"It's not to settle, just to earn enough so we're not living hand to mouth. I want to buy you pretty things."

Sure enough, she landed a job right off, from a Help Wanted sign on a dirty old red brick building that looked like it had moved from New Hampshire too. She was a Box Assembler-Machine Operator at minimum wage, forty hours a week. The foreman wanted to know if she could work overtime. She said yes, remembering all the money her dad threw around when he'd had a job with time and a half.

They rented a second-story flat with a kitchen in

the living room, but a separate bedroom. After Boston, they were used to a bathroom in the hall, and they didn't even have to share this one. There was a porch out back that overlooked a flower garden. She wished again for a camera to take a picture of this first real home of theirs.

Andy took to smoking cigarettes like Frenchy out on that porch while Regina watched *The Bill Cosby Show* and *Golden Girls* and *Cheers* on a little old black and white TV. Tired from working fifty or sixty hours a week, she'd sit and look at the flowers, smelling cut grass and car exhaust. Smoking, she'd run her hands along the new tight muscles in her upper arms. Regina had bought her a couple of black muscle shirts, one with a picture of Dolly Parton on it, the other with a German shepherd. After about a month, Andy figured they were enough ahead that she could get some new parts for the Studebaker, and she began fixing and polishing the old car till you couldn't tell it had ever left Weirs Beach.

One month turned to two, then to several, and Regina seemed content to keep house and shop. She'd turned out to be a pretty good cook, fixing canned ravioli less and less often and even learning to make Andy's favorite food, homemade baked beans, using Gramma's recipe that Ma sent. At a big bookstore nearby Regina bought used fat novels and she always had a stack by the couch.

Andy had never thought of herself as tall, but after almost a year of living with Regina, loving and being loved, her body had straightened, her shoulders had squared, and she'd stopped feeling like a small person.

On her twenty-second birthday Andy looked down

her own body and found that she'd lost her baby fat. She ran her hands over the angles and shadows that were her. Angular lines had begun to cut through her face, too, and hinted at her Dad's sharp cheekbones and jaw. Her hair had grown longer so it curled rakishly at her collar, and she combed those shaggy bangs off to the side, into a hank of hair that was always falling into her eyes. Regina sometimes tenderly brushed it aside, calling her "my shaggy-craggy loverwoman."

"People still stare at me on the street, but maybe Columbus is just where we belong," she said to Regina, who'd fixed her Frenchy-style spaghetti and decorated a cake for her birthday. She'd also given her an inexpensive personal radio with headset so she could listen to the country/western station at work.

"I feel like I'm on vacation, Andy. Like I've been climbing mountains all my life and now I can just live like everybody else."

"Yeah."

Delighted in Regina, Andy no longer scowled relentlessly. Even out in the world, she could feel that new, infatuated kid-grin take over her lips no matter how hard she tried to suppress it. Walking down the street with a skip and a lilt, no longer trying to avoid notice, she'd laugh aloud, at last unafraid to be heard, to be in the world. Any time teenaged boys started to cut up about her looks she'd pretend she was Frenchy, bowing her legs and adding a challenging bounce to her walk as well as a thrust to her chin. She'd dredge up her scowl as a last resort and they'd usually shut up.

"It's so hot," Regina said one night, stretched out

on the porch chaise lounge, fanning herself with a novel.

Andy wanted to pass her hand up the gap between Regina's shorts and her thigh, right up to that hot, wet, curly place so she could see Regina shudder with pleasure. Then they'd go inside and"

"Remember that air-conditioned roadhouse we passed on the way to the store?" Regina asked.

"With the big neon sign?"

Regina laughed. "Looked a little like Broadway, didn't it?"

The mention of New York City still scared Andy. "What about it?"

"I'd love to just go sit there some evenings."

Andy didn't let herself look at the wet-lipped pout. "We can't save money to move on if we start going to bars."

"Don't we have enough yet? We've been here a long time."

"Almost," said Andy, though she knew they could leave tonight if they continued to be thrifty. "We can do one or the other, use up the money or save it."

"Maybe I ought to get a job."

"You know that's not such a good idea."

Regina slept on the couch that night, claiming it was too hot with the two of them in bed.

A shudder passed through Andy's sweaty body when they first entered the cold roadhouse. She'd broken down and taken Regina there, knowing there'd be the devil to pay, as Gramma would say. She called her folks now and then, but they only talked about the weather and how her two little brothers were growing. Gramma had been with her more and more in her head, telling her what to do at work and at home, just like Frenchy told her what to do on the street.

Of course she and Regina couldn't dance together. She had to content herself with slumping in the booth, smoking, letting the beer she didn't want go flat on the formica table before her, while she watched Regina dance with the men who all seemed to look like Roy. Regina's five earrings sparkled under the colored lights that hung from the ceiling. The hot spell kept up, so one night wasn't enough.

"Go ahead home without me, Sweet Andy," Regina said one night, as Andy had known she would. "I know you're tired. One of the boys will bring me up the road."

There was just something in Regina that wanted those men to admire her.

"No," said Andy, straightening, thinking of the boss in Boston. "I can't sleep without you in the bed."

Regina's eyes flashed anger, but she replaced it with cunning.

If Regina thought she would wear Andy down, it hadn't worked. Andy refused to go back to the roadhouse. Regina sulked for a few days, then began to smile again. She'd come back to bed, and now she became gentle and liked all the touches she'd first taught Andy. No longer did she want this or that complicated maneuver that Andy liked so little she'd no longer be in the mood. This was making love for real.

"You're so good to me, Andy," Regina said. "I like you so much. Life is sweet with you around. Don't ever let me mess this up. Please," she begged. "I want to be happy and peaceful like this forever."

CHAPTER FIVE

At first Verne only came in the daytime. Andy was glad Regina had a friend, something to do besides read all day. Then Verne went on days at the college lab and began to come over at night, the time Andy and Regina usually spent together.

Verne was a little taller than she was, with broad shoulders and neat black hair. Andy thought she was kind of show-offy, wearing her white pantsuit uniform over to the house all the time, but then she came from a snooty well-off family that was so mad at her for being gay they wouldn't pay for her schooling. Andy cut her a lot of slack. Her girlfriend, Cressa, was pretty, black and sarcastic. Andy had a hard time knowing when she was joking and felt dumb around her. Regina, Verne and Cressa would play Pictionary and Trivial Pursuit. Andy had no patience with games, especially as tired as she felt with all the overtime.

She was paid for machine assembly work, but found out that the company never had to hire mechanics because you couldn't get your production out if you didn't learn quick to make your machine work. So after six days a week of running and fixing machines that were held together with baling wire, while the company waited for the government's economic miracles to help them retool, she'd be exhausted and wild to get outdoors.

Even at home the Columbus air smelled of factory smoke, but it was late spring again and Andy would go out on the back porch to watch the stars and satellites twinkle in the Ohio sky, and wonder if they were the same ones she'd known back in New Hampshire.

She was on the porch the night Regina and her friends played strip poker. She could hear the ballgame on the TV. When she went inside later for her cigarettes she wished she'd never admired Frenchy enough to start smoking. There sat Verne, bare-chested, a high color on her face, dealing cards. Cressa was in her bra and panties. For once no smart-aleck sayings flew out of her mouth when Andy appeared. Regina wore nothing on top either. She was leaning over Verne's broad shoulder to pour her some beer. There was a feeling in the room that reminded Andy of her early days with Regina, when they would just dance together and she didn't imagine that there was more two women could do.

Except this also felt like one of those new bed tricks Regina used to think up. Or something she might have learned with one of her Roys. It felt dirty and made her mad. Did she have any right to be mad or was this what gay people did? If it was all right to be angry, what should she do about it? She couldn't just stand there and stare at them; Cressa would make fun of her. Why wasn't there anyone to ask what to do? She picked up her cigarettes and her anger and took them outside. One thing she knew for sure, she wouldn't want to be the kind of gay woman Verne was.

After a while Cressa joined her with a lit cigarette and a beer. She was wearing Regina's robe and Andy could tell there wasn't a thing under it. She moved her legs so Cressa could use the other chair. Her tongue was burned with the hot nasty nicotine taste of cigarette after cigarette.

"What do you do out here all the time?"

"Look at the stars."

"Wouldn't you rather be with us?"

Andy smiled down at the gray-painted wooden floorboards. Cressa was being unusually nice. "I'm no good at games," she answered softly.

"Seems like I'm not either tonight. It's just Verne and Regina now. I wish you'd stopped it when you came in before."

Andy squinted at the stars. "I didn't know what to do."

"The stakes got too high for me when we ran out of clothes and started betting gals. I almost won you." She peered through the dark at Andy's puzzled face. "Regina won an hour alone with Verne. They're in there now doing it, I'll bet."

"No," said Andy with the same jolt of fear she'd felt when she thought Regina might stay in New York. Cressa must be teasing her again. She looked into her face and saw a reflection of her own pain.

"I wouldn't let it happen, but Verne doesn't stop at hitting when I get in her way. So I'll stay out of her way for an hour. Any longer than that, though, I don't know if I can stand it. I love that woman."

There was a pain in Andy's gut so bad she'd never felt anything like it before. It was worse than taunts on the street, worse than the boss at the coffee shop, worse than the dancing men at the roadhouse. It didn't matter that Regina would later be sorry and cry in her arms, wishing she weren't so evil. The pain was so bad it stood Andy up and pushed her toward the apartment before she could worry about being right.

But she was afraid to see Regina with Verne.

She stood in the doorway rooted, swaying in silent pain. The anger inside her was pushed down by the fear.

"I know how you feel," said Cressa with a sorrowful tone. "It's freaky seeing them touch like that."

And then Andy shot forward, her anger released because Cressa was hurting too.

Andy saw it all like a picture in a newspaper. In the bedroom Regina and Verne were on the bed together. The lamp shone in their eyes like a flashbulb. Verne's two wet, guilty fingers were stopped still, about to reenter Regina. Her breasts were in Regina's hands, just like Andy's had been so often, and Andy felt embarrassed that Verne would know Regina did this to her, she did this to Regina.

There was no sound from the room for a full minute, yet Regina's mouth stayed open, in a little "o," about to make the cry Andy knew so well. Regina had been ready to drown. *I'm drowning, Andy,* Regina always sang. *Save me, Andy,* she would plead so Andy would know it was time to go inside her faster and faster until Regina breathed, *My hero,* and then they'd lie together, so happy.

The whole room smelled like Regina down there. Andy grabbed Verne's sweaty upper arm. She hauled Verne up off the bed, but Verne lost her balance and fell, knocking Andy down. Looking up at the naked Verne, Andy felt her anger slide out of her like air out of a balloon. She didn't want to hurt Verne now that she'd stopped the source of her own, and Cressa's, pain.

When they had dressed, Verne and Cressa left. Cressa mouthed a thank you at Andy on the porch. Andy crumpled her half pack of cigarettes until there was nothing left but shreds and filters. Smoking wasn't for her.

Regina called from the bedroom, "They gone, Sweet Andy? Come in here, my red-headed lover."

She silenced the TV with a savage twist. Then she looked at Regina from the doorway, lying on their bed. She was relieved it was over, but didn't feel good. She leaned against the doorjamb, hands hidden in her back pockets.

"Touch me, lover," Regina said, and Andy, still numb with shock, did, putting her hand like Regina said on the wetness Verne had just left. Regina pulled at her, and Andy fought her own revulsion. It wasn't over at all. She was just finishing what Verne had started.

"You know I was just fooling around, Andy," Regina said, moving against her, drawing her closer. "It didn't mean a thing. Not like with you."

Andy's head cleared then. She withdrew her hand and stood, backing away from the bed.

She could see worry in Regina's eyes, but Regina's body was still pleading. Didn't she care who it was she —

There was no word of Verne for almost two weeks after that. Then Andy came home the night before payday to find that Regina had bought beer and other supplies for a party on credit at the bologna and Wonderbread store where she shopped frequently.

"We haven't had any fun for weeks!" Regina said to her protests. "Just stop in on your way home tomorrow and pay them."

Andy knew that tone. She made their dinner while Regina put her makeup on. She wondered if Regina would have been better off working after all.

Verne was at the party, without Cressa, and a few other women were there who made Andy stutter and finally not talk at all. Twice Andy saw Verne touch Regina in ways that made her sure that Verne, who had her days off when Andy worked, had been hanging around. The smells and strange hairs in the bed weren't something Andy could ignore any longer. Regina put her gentle hands on Verne too, drawing her to her, pushing her away. It was like watching Regina and herself in the early days. It seemed like Regina just couldn't stand to be too good. Was she scared of her own good side?

By the next morning, Regina hadn't come to bed. She wasn't on the couch either. There was nothing but a note. *I love you, Sweet Andy, but I have to go. Find a woman who's good enough for you. Love, R.*

Andy only went to the box factory that day to get her paycheck. She was so anxious to get home again that she didn't even stop to cash it. Hope pounded in her chest till it hurt. She raced up the stairs and fumbled with the lock, then slammed the door open. The apartment was still empty. Regina was really gone, along with all her new clothes and makeup. She'd left nothing but the fat books which Andy held in her lap all evening. She stared at the front door, wishing it would open, not letting herself cry in case Regina, in case her life, came walking back through the door.

At 10:00 p.m. she gave up. The apartment was too empty to sleep in. She packed her clothes and the few mechanics' tools and manuals she'd managed to collect and put them in that old Studebaker. She had twenty dollars in her pocket, enough to fill up the car, and she decided she'd worry about eating if ever she got hungry again.

She stopped at the automatic teller to get enough money to pay the grocery store. She'd take half of their $356 savings since she'd earned it. The machine took her card all right, but when she tried to make a withdrawal it said the funds weren't in there. She started sweating, not wanting to believe what must have happened. For the first time fear shook her very center. After trying three times she realized that Regina must have taken it out already. At first that gave her hope. Regina wouldn't run off with all their money. Maybe she was planning to come back.

Or maybe she assumed Andy would have the whole two-week paycheck for herself, about the same amount. Regina wasn't coming back. But Andy couldn't deposit the check because the machine wouldn't give her anything. Should she wait till Monday to leave? As if anything was worth waiting for now.

Should she go home to New Hampshire? How could she go there? She'd always been a sore thumb, like Frenchy said, and now she, and everyone else in town, knew why. Should she head across the country like she'd planned with Regina and hope to get a job in the next state? Should she try to find Regina? She grew more numb every minute.

Leaning against the shelf in a half phone booth that smelled bad, she called Frenchy.

"No, kid, Regina didn't show up here."

She told Frenchy about Verne.

"There always is another woman, isn't there?" Frenchy sighed as if she'd been through this too. Andy wished she could talk to her. "Where's the other woman from?"

"I think Regina's party was for Verne's graduation. Then she was going home to Chicago."

"Look for them there, Andy. I think you're right. Regina would've headed down here if she was in the city."

She spat out the window of the Studebaker as she hit the highway ramp. So Columbus hadn't been safe either. Would any place be?

CHAPTER SIX

Andy scowled through her windshield. For as far as she could see out the window of that old Studebaker, the fields were planted with corn. The silent twilight smelled of richly irrigated earth. She was so hungry she wondered if it would help to steal a tasteless unripe ear and gnaw on it.

"That'll give you collywobbles, Andy Blaine," she heard her Gramma softly chide her from the long gone past.

Though she'd never in her twenty-two years

found out what collywobbles were, she certainly didn't need them on top of everything else. Besides, gas prices were well over a dollar a gallon and she still wouldn't have enough money to fill the Studebaker's tank. That, more than her own hunger, made her break down and cry hard for the first time since Gramma went and died on her when she was seven. She could smell Gramma's Jergens Hand Lotion right now in the car.

Night was coming in slowly, like it wasn't relishing the heat. Willie Nelson sang "You've Been On My Mind" over and over in her head. She sat sniffing and sobbing until she had to find a rag. She bent over her trunk for a long time, forgetting what she was looking for. The familiar oily smell of the rag made her cry worse. She hadn't worked with any car but her own since she'd left New Hampshire. She spat to get the oil taste out of her mouth.

June of 1989, she thought. Same month, same week, almost the same day Regina left, but it felt like a century had passed. Why had Regina gone? Was something so wrong with her she'd driven her away? Just when she thought she'd found the answer to everything by finding out she was gay, she was back to square one, wondering what it was all about. Even her gay lover wanted nothing to do with her.

Was there a way to go back to not being gay? But Frenchy had said she'd even been a gay kid. Andy was stuck with it, like a marked woman.

She caught an early firefly and held it like a warm light in her hand before she let it go. She wished she at least had a picture of herself and

Regina in that old Studebaker, some remnant of Regina besides this pain. Something to say it had all been worthwhile.

Hellishly hot, she'd rolled up her windows in the 2:00 a.m. chill last night and felt baked by 11:00. She'd slept like she never wanted to be conscious again. And she was sorry when she was. As soon as she came full awake the clamoring memories pounded in her head. The fiery pain had raged in her every minute since then. She inhaled pain, exhaled pain, sweated pain, had driven all day in pain — wanted to yell in pain now, out the window into the hushed cornfield. Instead she beat the steering wheel with her fists. What good was life? She'd begun to believe in herself, in her own dream of a place where she wouldn't be odd girl out all the time. She'd believed in Regina, in their love, in the home they'd planned.

Was Regina all the dirty dishonest things she seemed to know about, like turning everything into sex, and wanting men even though she said she was gay, and lying? Gramma would say, "There're plenty more fish in the sea."

"But there's another side to her," she told a new firefly, as if it were Gramma. "She's sweet and trusting, even if she did only show it to me, like she was ashamed when she wasn't as tough as nails."

Andy let the firefly go and climbed back into the car. She slouched there, her stomach growling. The muggy Indiana twilight put a film of sweat on her forehead and she wiped it off, wishing for a long shower. Her stomach growled louder. Hadn't Regina dropped some coins in the car last time they'd gone for a Sunday ride? She reached into the grit under the front seat. One quarter. Another. A penny.

She'd stopped not far from a Holiday Inn. Hiking toward it, the gravel on the shoulder of the road loud and bumpy under her worn Nikes, she fingered the two quarters. The restaurant menu was posted. She couldn't even afford a cup of tea, but she spotted vending machines and spent a long time weighing the merits of a bag of peanuts against a chocolate-covered coconut bar. In the newspaper machine the headline said that Iran's fanatic leader, the Ayatollah Khomeini, had died. It was a shock to realize that the world still spun.

The hot water in the motel restaurant's bathroom felt so good and homey on her face, the gooey liquid soap smelled so much like a pretty woman, that she almost cried again.

When she looked in the mirror, though, and saw her own light blue eyes wild and desperate under her uncombed coppery hair, she knew she was far from any home she'd ever had or ever would have.

Home again, home again, jiggety-jig, Gramma used to chant.

She was cut loose. The way it was supposed to work, once you found your own true love, you stayed together through thick and thin. She might not have had the greatest family in the world, but at least her mom and dad had stuck it out. They fought like cats and dogs, but every Saturday night they'd leave the little boys with Andy and go down to one of the bars at the beach to horse around the dance floor with a few beers under their belts. All she'd wanted was to make money doing what she was good at, to keep that old Studebaker in shape, to laugh with Regina and to take her out on Saturday nights. It hadn't seemed like a lot to ask.

She walked back to the car. A pickup whizzed by, leaving a hot breeze and the sound of crickets in its wake. There was one little bird peeping its soul into the night. The cornfield was absolutely motionless until darkness finally settled in with a hot breeze that seemed like a sigh.

When the peeping bird woke her, searing pain swept into her limbs, her heart, her thoughts. She judged by the moon that it was only about 11:00 p.m., a long time till morning when she could look for a way to make some money.

How could she do anything? She felt so heavy with sadness she'd never be able to sit up, much less work. How could she cut Regina out of her life like a bruise on an apple? What do you do when somebody just walks away with your happiness? She'd rather not live than have to feel this pain.

She woke from a nightmare and reached for Regina, but her arm leapt back from the empty space beside her as if from a shock. She lay in the dark gripping herself until she hurt from the dents her fingernails made in her arms, and this time let herself howl into the hot Indiana night, howl into her tiny shelter, howl into the emptiness that had once been their lives together. She remembered their first whole night, doing it in the Studebaker in Boston, how she'd wanted Regina as much as she now mourned her.

Where was she? She'd had in mind fleeing all the way across the country, not stopping until she hit Oregon, straight across the map from New

Hampshire. There she'd fix up old cars and take photographs of them. The pictures would be so beautiful they'd be put in a Chicago museum. Regina would see them and come back to her.

A shadow fell over the Studebaker. "See your license, sir."

CHAPTER SEVEN

Andy jumped, disoriented, frightened. The state trooper had come up so quietly. Or had she fallen asleep again? She fumbled for her wallet.

"Ma'am, I mean," said the trooper as he inspected her license. He smelled of pipe tobacco. "Sorry. Long way from home, aren't you?"

Andy looked at his jacket to remind herself. Indiana. "Yes, sir. Just getting some rest before I drive on to Chicago."

"Good idea." He took her license and registration, but soon was back. "There's a church parking lot up a way, ma'am. Just follow all the road signs toward town. It'll be safer for you there. And this is private property." He began to leave but stopped, an admiring smile replacing the blank face he'd been showing her. "Great car," he said, and strode off.

Andy turned the key in the ignition and began to drive, hoping she could get out before he checked to see if she had money, a place to go — if she was an undesirable. That's exactly what she felt like, an undesirable. Regina didn't want her, that was plain. The trooper would throw her in the hoosegow, as Gramma would say, if he knew she was gay and chasing a woman.

Not that being married was any bed of roses from what she could see. "You don't think I'm going to take your philandering sitting down, do you?" her mother had screamed at her dad. They drank together Saturdays, but there were other nights in the week. "You think I can't smell that dame's perfume? Can't see her lipstick on you?"

"Pipe down, Kitty. I was only fooling around. You're my best girl," her dad would claim, trying to get an arm around her mom.

The next morning, Dad off at the garage, Andy's brother Everett, who was eleven, said, "Why don't you just take off on the bastard, Ma?"

Her mom smacked Everett. "Don't call him names! He's your dad, whatever he does. And he's my husband. That means I stick with him through thick or thin. When he wants me, when he doesn't want me, and all the times in between. It's just like they say, for better or worse. Nobody's perfect, least of all me." Whatever her folks had, Andy wouldn't turn it down.

She wanted to reach Regina before it was too late. Wasn't she *supposed* to be saving their love? Maybe it was only the love between women and men that was worth saving.

Or maybe she'd missed the boat somewhere. Regina had talked about how great their lives would be together, but had she also said she *wasn't* happy? Were there people who didn't like to be happy? What good was it to be gay if it hurt so much?

She looked at the fields along the road. The bugs and mice, the corn, the birds, rabbits and maybe even deer — each must think it was the most important thing in the world, just like she did. No matter how bad she felt, no matter even if she died of her grief, all those bugs and rabbits and birds, they'd keep on flying and eating and building nests anyhow. It wasn't that she didn't count in the world, but she and her little troubles didn't make any more of a dent than theirs.

What did it matter if she got to Chicago and begged for Regina's love, or if she got squashed against a windshield like some bug? What was the big deal about being gay or being straight?

She looked at the tooled metal pattern on her silver dashboard. She touched the beautiful silver hawk on her horn, the classy red upholstery against the black of the body. Regina had looked so beautiful in her car. She'd never want anyone but her so she might as well give up being gay. Who needed love anyway? She kept driving.

Route 39 was straight and unlit. Moths flashed like fools before her windshield and then were gone.

The night was cooler and the sweet scent of a newly mown field reminded her of home. Because she hadn't eaten much, everything looked funny. Was that something in the road ahead? An animal? She slowed. The darn thing was just lying in the middle of the road like it was waiting for her. She honked. It stayed right there. It wasn't dead, was it? She couldn't stand any more pain.

"You darn fool," she said, getting out of her car and walking to the thin, scruffy white mutt with brown spots like mud puddles. It had the longest, scraggliest ears she'd ever seen on a living being. "I can't even figure out what to do with my worthless old self and here I suppose you want me to take care of you."

In the glare from her headlights she stood over the dog and watched its tail thump like it was glad Andy had finally gotten there. After she petted it her hand smelled like dirty dog.

"What's your problem, dog?"

It thumped faster.

"Get up now. Get over to the other side of the darn road. I can't take you with me."

The dog stood and looked at her with absolute love in its eyes.

"So you're a girl." She reached down to scratch its neck. "How come you haven't got any collar? Don't you belong anywhere either?" She licked Andy's hand. It felt good to be touched. "You are one horse's ass of a dog, you know that?"

Andy walked back to her car. She squeezed quickly inside. Another car appeared in her rearview mirror, coming on fast. There was no time to get the dog out of the way and she felt sick at the thought of it being squashed —

It wasn't hit. It wagged its tail, waiting, really cute with those dangling ears.

"You are a lucky horse's ass, I'll give you that."

Maybe she should take her to the nearest farmhouse. No, she couldn't do that at this time of night. Maybe she should tie her to a tree. But if no one untied her, the dog would starve. She'd have to go around her.

As usual, that old Studebaker started like a dream. She backed away from the dog, not wanting to leave her behind. There was an empty place in her heart, wasn't there? An empty seat beside her? Another car came toward them. Andy froze. The dog *was* lucky. She just stood there, sadly watching, as if she knew Andy was going about things all backwards as usual.

Andy laughed. *I could call her Clover.*

She and Gramma had always looked for four-leaf clovers back home. Maybe she'd had to travel all the way to Indiana to find this dumb four-legged Clover, to find some luck, something to make her life a little easier to get through.

"Oh, damn," she said, shifting gears, the first smile since Regina left taking over her face. "It can't hurt to love you."

She rolled to a stop. She opened the door to let the dog jump over her lap and onto the seat. Clover lay right down, leaning her muzzle across Andy's thigh, eyes full of devotion. Andy touched Clover's head, stroked her ears. The dog licked her again.

Andy didn't want to smile. "Well, you're not Regina," she said. "But you'll do."

CHAPTER EIGHT

There wasn't a light on in the buildings, but the streetlights lit up pools of detail.

Andy watched Clover's brown patches rise and fall as the dog slept. Hunger pangs shot through her as she wondered how to feed *both* of them. What now, Gramma?

Old Mother Hubbard/Went to the cupboard,/To fetch her poor dog a bone;/But when she got there/The cupboard was bare,/And so the poor dog had none.

Maybe in the morning — But one idea was more

useless than the last. Nothing would change by daylight. She'd still, as Dad would say, railing against the gay libbers and their parades, be queer as a three-dollar bill. All she wanted to be was an honest, hard-working, small-town person.

She had an urge for a cigarette, but remembered the terrible taste of her last one the night of the strip poker game. She was glad she wouldn't have to use her money for those things. She'd just wanted to be more like Frenchy, really gay and good at life. Cigarettes hadn't worked. Probably she just wasn't cut out to be a lesbian. She'd be better off staying away from women. No one knew her in Indiana. She could get a fresh start.

She turned the radio on softly to cheer herself up, avoiding sad country/western songs. But on the rock station Tracy Chapman sang "Fast Car." How she and Regina had loved that song, sung it at the top of their lungs out the Studebaker's windows as they fled Weirs Beach thigh to thigh. She roughly turned off the radio. There wasn't a thing she thought about that didn't bring Regina to mind. Why had that woman just kept acting worse the more Andy loved her?

Gramma, why aren't you here to help me? You died and they started having those little boys I had to take care of. Why was she thinking of Gramma so much? Regina went away and Gramma came back. Was that how it worked?

Okay, Andy thought, what would I do if Gramma were sitting beside me hungry and thirsty and dirty and we had no money? I'd get her food and a root beer and a bathroom.

Back home, she thought, where there was a

town, there was water. The lake, a river, ocean, even a brook.

She opened the door and slipped out, pausing for Clover to join her. The dog didn't stir.

"Clover," she whispered.

Nothing.

She looked around. No one was in earshot. "Clover," she said louder.

The dog's long ears didn't even twitch.

Andy didn't dare shout, so she leaned across the seat and tapped Clover on the shoulder. The dog was up and out the door, tail wagging, in seconds.

They set off toward some clumps of trees strung out across the horizon. It was still cool, and green things underfoot gave off rich clean scents as she walked. She began to feel as if she were the boss, darn it, not Regina or the uncaring world. In the dark she tripped once or twice, but Clover guided her.

After a few minutes she heard Clover's tongue lapping. Andy lay on her stomach and scooped handfuls of the cold rushing water to her mouth. They both rolled onto their backs, bellies bloated with water, on the dark bank of the stream. Clover's dirty paws stuck straight up as she scratched her back, wiggling this way and that. Andy finally led them up the bank, her body aching all over. She fell asleep once more under a tree.

When she woke to the sunrise she felt light-headed, but her mind was as clear as the sky. She was buoyant with hope as she rolled down the hill to the water and drank again.

Buying a toothbrush and paste would be one of

the first things she'd do — she could kick herself for forgetting them — but for now she chewed on some mint leaves that grew along the stream. She was just a woman from New Hampshire, not queer as a three-dollar bill, not dumped by her girlfriend, a clean slate. Clover loved her. They'd find their way in the world just fine, starting this morning.

The area was isolated. She stripped off her clothes, top first, then more daringly, her work pants, and bathed the best she could in the stream. Regina had always used a perfumed soap, but the stream had a clean, new smell to it Andy welcomed. The cold rocks under her feet felt refreshingly uncomfortable, the wet splashing on her private parts made them hers again.

Clover chased waterbugs the whole time, snapping at them with her long jaws as if they would make a sufficient breakfast.

"Clover!" she called when she was dry and dressed again. "Clover!" She stood just on the edge of the stream.

But Clover didn't come. Andy studied this dog. Hadn't she ever had people who trained her to answer? She walked to Clover and led her up the bank by the wet scruff of her neck. She smelled like a wool sweater on a rainy day.

As a kid, Andy had teased the neighbor dog by whistling real high. His ears would stand up in a comical way. When she whistled high at Clover nothing happened. The dog didn't seem to notice.

Clover cocked her head to one side as if trying to read her mind.

Hopeful, Andy shouted, "Clover?" The dog's head

was still bent. Maybe she was hard of hearing only in one ear. "Clover! Clover! Clover!" Andy yelled, lifting first one ear, then the other.

"All those ears and you can't hear a thing, can you? I never heard of a damn deaf dog before." Andy collapsed back onto the grass. She looked pityingly at the dog. Clover moved closer and licked up and down her face. Andy laughed and hugged her, wet as the dog was. "Every time I'm feeling bad you're going to remind me, aren't you, girl. You get along just fine stone deaf and I'll get along too."

They started back toward town. It was almost like being with Regina again, someone with a whole side of herself that needed protection. Would it hurt just as much if the dog left her?

Deaf or not, love wouldn't feed the dog. They stopped to check on that old Studebaker, then walked onto the main street. She carried her uncashed paycheck, but no banks would cash it. She saw a thrift store. Maybe they'd know how to help. The shop was small, but light and clean. Behind the register a big moon-faced woman sat so erect she looked like she was on a throne, waiting for Andy to bow. She grimaced at Clover.

"Please, miss," said Andy. "Clover's deaf. I don't like to leave her outside."

The woman said nothing. Andy imagined what she must think of this bedraggled overgrown gay child in men's work clothes. What did it matter? Andy had sworn off women.

"We're from out of town," Andy said, stuttering. "We don't have any food or money and the car's about out of gas. Is there someone who can help us? I'm a good strong worker."

Clover had meanwhile presented her rump to the woman.

"Your poor doggie hasn't eaten?" she asked. The woman shook all her bracelets further up her arm before giving Clover a good scratch. "I've got fourteen pups of my own," she said. A proud smile softened her face.

"Fourteen?"

"I breed Salukis," she said with a laugh. "And I know what it costs to feed those big mouths!" She felt inside an immense black pocketbook and her eyes narrowed. "Why did you bring your dog along wherever you're going if you can't feed her?"

"I didn't exactly bring her. She kind of picked me up." Andy blushed. Regina would have teased her for using that expression, but the lady didn't seem to think along those lines. "I have my paycheck too, but no place to cash it yet."

"Would a roast beef sandwich do?"

"Oh, we couldn't take your lunch."

"Don't be silly. I'll have Willa, my daughter, run me down another one on her way to work."

"But —"

"Be proud for yourself, young woman. Let your dog eat."

Andy took the sandwich.

"And give it to her outside. I don't want her deciding this is a Roy Rogers Restaurant for doggies. Then take yourselves down to that church on the corner. This shop is Reverend Carrier's idea. Tell him Mrs. Kohl sent you."

They went outside and around a corner into the shade. Squatting, she gave half the sandwich to Clover. Nothing had ever tasted as good to her as those thin scraps of over-cooked beef in a bath of mayonnaise. This wasn't bad, bumming around the country with her dog. Or wouldn't be if the jagged pain that came every time she thought of Regina would lay off.

She sat there for a while, arm around Clover. It was pretty here. Maybe they'd find a little place cheap and set up housekeeping, her and Clover. Things had been peaceful in Weirs Beach before Regina. She'd gone fishing with her brothers and spent a lot of time over at Elma's, her 75-year-old friend who was housebound. Her best friend in high school, Jeannie, was married and had three children. Jeannie had been a homely practical joker when they'd sat together on the bus to the regional high school. Sometimes Andy would take her and the kids over to Meredith window shopping, or she'd drive them to a playground and watch Jeannie play tricks that delighted the little kids.

She stood and brushed off her work pants. Like Dad would say, she wouldn't get far sitting on her butt. He'd told her that when she hadn't wanted to leave his shop. He'd taught her everything she knew about being a mechanic and she'd been willing to stay on for just room and board. Dad said he wanted her to be out on her own, to find work a woman should be doing. But she knew it was because her brother Everett was starting high school. He was already costing room and board and Dad put him to work. There wasn't enough for all of them to do.

Though she'd parked right behind the church, it hadn't occurred to her to go there for help. She hadn't ever had much use for churches. Hell and brimstone had never helped anyone she knew, but she didn't have a whole lot of choices. Even though she was a good mechanic, if women's lib hadn't hit Weirs Beach, New Hampshire or Boston, Massachusetts, could she hope it had hit Indiana? Even so, there must be a car wash, an auto body shop or a box factory in the town.

The minister's small white house had filmy curtains billowing out with the breeze. His wife, when she answered the door, looked kind of like those curtains, like the wind would blow her around just as easily. Women's lib hadn't hit her for sure. She eyed Andy's muddy feet and asked her to wait on the porch.

Andy was almost asleep on the soft cushions of the wicker chair by the time the minister — short, with thick sandy hair — appeared. He gave her hand a hearty shake.

She talked in her shy gruff voice, trying not to stutter, hands wringing themselves. She told him the whole story except about being gay. And she hoped, with every word, she would never have to go begging like this again. She'd stay out of messes, walk away from the Roys, wait to cash her paychecks, forget about being gay. Who needed it?

"All I need is a start."

"Why," said the minister, "don't we start with lunch for you and your dog then?"

Had Gramma somehow led her to this place? Andy was so grateful that she cried right there in front of the minister.

CHAPTER NINE

By nightfall, when stars began to show in the clear sky, Andy had a room over the minister's garage, two good meals under her belt, and a ten-dollar tab to pay off at the thrift store for new clothes, dishes, bedding, an alarm clock and a big red collar for Clover.

She'd played for a long time with a dusty camera on the shelf behind Mrs. Kohl.

"That's one of your classic cameras there, an Argus," Mrs. Kohl had said. "It may use the old-fashioned flashbulbs, but it never takes a bad picture. See? The instructions are still with it. It's worth a lot more than seven-fifty."

"Let me make sure I can cash this check. I'd like to buy it."

"I'll put it away for you then, and add one dollar to your bill to hold it."

Andy started work the next morning, doing long overdue repairs at the church and parsonage.

If Gramma hadn't led her here, then Clover had brought her good luck. Reverend Carrier was a different kind of minister. He seemed really to believe that he could be in her situation as easily as anyone.

At the end of the day she tied Clover on a rope outside the garage and went to the parsonage for a bath. That was the only problem. There was nothing but an old outhouse for the garage apartment.

She scrubbed the sweat and grime off, looking at her body, slick with a soap Regina had never used. Andy had long legs, but wasn't tall, and she loved the muscles in her upper arms and the prominent veins in her forearms and hands. Soon the box factory paper cuts on her hands would heal. Regina had said her breasts were just right, a handful each, and had gone into ecstasies the first time she'd seen Andy's wild thatch of red hair. She reached down there to pat it like a beloved kitten, but stopped, remembering that she was in a minister's house.

Would Regina ever touch her there again? Any woman? Even if she wasn't going to be gay any more she didn't want a man touching her.

Clover was outside, upset by the bath Andy had given her earlier, and impatient at being tied. Andy bent to hug her. "Don't you turn into Oscar the

Grouch. I'm trying to protect you," she said. "The world doesn't care much about dogs' lives. People are supposed to be most important, but it's even hard for some of us to be safe."

They sat on the edge of the bed, upstairs in the garage that smelled faintly of mildew, looking out the window across the fields. Here she was, like all those people she'd learned about in the history books, hiding out in a church. Had the world ever been safe?

There was a song Gramma sang — she'd never realized how much she remembered, or how much Gramma must have had sung and read and recited to her. *The north wind doth blow,/And we shall have snow,/And what will poor robin do then,/Poor thing?/He'll sit in a barn,/To keep himself warm,/And hide his head under his wing,/Poor thing!*

There'd been a time without cars, when roads did not cut through every bit of natural land. There'd been a time when no one killed animals except for food. Had there been a time when love didn't hurt? When her kind of love was allowed?

A fly dove through the window with a maddening buzz. Clover wanted it. She swiveled her head this way and that, trying to snap at it. She looked so comical Andy laughed. Her laughter built and built, watching this silly creature who looked like one of those spring-necked, floppy-eared dogs in the backs of cars bobbing up and down.

"Come on, girl," she said when the fly had escaped out the window. She got under the worn, but soft and clean comforter she'd bought for a dollar. It felt like heaven and smelled like home. She curled around Clover's soft body and pushed Regina from her mind.

For two weeks she worked around the church until she was running out of things to do and worrying that she'd have to leave. She was working in the front yard, cleaning out the brambles and crabgrass that had gotten out of hand, when an ancient Chevrolet pulled up to the curb.

"The Rev tells me you're the owner of that Studebaker," said the driver. He must have been fifty, and wore a gas station uniform. "Wonder if I could look at it?"

She was always glad to show off her car.

The man looked for a long time — at the body, the exhaust system, and under the hood. "I hear you're short on cash."

She just looked at him, feeling an ominous scowl coming on. She pulled off her work gloves and dried her palms on her overalls.

"I wonder if you'd like to sell."

Andy folded her arms. She wanted to yank the guy out of her driver's seat. "No."

"Oh, well." He sighed and got out. "No harm in asking."

The next day he came by again and offered her $500 for the car.

A few days later, $850.

She could see he loved that old Studebaker as much as she did, and softened toward him a little, even telling him that she admired his Chevy. After she'd turned down the $850, he introduced himself. He owned a gas station just outside of town.

"The Reverend says you do good work, Andy. And fool with cars a little."

"I have some of my own tools, too," she replied.

"I hate like heck to steal you from him, but I just lost a fella to the service. You think you'd like a job pumping gas?"

Her heart raced. "You'd hire me for your station?"

"If *I* can't have that old Studebaker," he explained with a gleam of respect in his eyes, "I'd like to help keep her running. You can't do that without money."

She started pumping gas the next day, part-time. *If Regina could see me now,* she thought, then shushed her mind. That was all over except for the drag in her feet she felt when she tried to do three fill-ups and a two-dollar order at once. She had to force herself to race around. Days when she had no work at the church, she'd hang out and help the mechanic. She'd squirreled away all she could from the box factory check to rent a place as soon as she could, but with her first gas station paycheck she and Clover zoomed into town and stormed the thrift shop.

"I can pay my bill," she said. "And buy the camera."

Mrs. Kohl reached behind her, carefully peeled the taped sign that read *Sold — Blaine* from the camera and gave it to her. She filled her first roll of film with that old Studebaker and Clover, bitterly glad that she had no painful pictures of Regina to look at.

One day when it was full summer and hot, she ran the water hose over herself and Clover and they went to lie in the shade under an old tree between the station and the motel next door. She was watching the cars go by when a young woman lay down beside her, a big smile on her moon-face.

"Hi, Andy. I feel like I know you already. My mom runs the church thrift store in town and she told me all about you. And that floppy-eared dog of yours. I work over here at the motel. How're you getting on?"

Andy liked her right off because she did all the talking and was as homely as her old friend Jeannie. Willa, who was eighteen, started coming by every afternoon after she finished cleaning rooms. Andy would buy them both Cokes and they'd listen to the little portable radio Willa carried from room to room while she worked. When she got the first roll of film developed, Willa exclaimed over the shots of the car and dog as if they were fit to hang in a museum.

Later, Andy would recall those early afternoons with a special fondness. She and Clover and Willa, the three of them so small on the huge flat land, would sit under the one big tree left up on the town's commercial strip. Willa would talk lazily, trying to catch a breeze, listening to Willie Nelson and K.T. Oslin on the little radio.

"You seem so sad, Andy," Willa was always telling her. Andy ached to tell Willa about Regina, but she swallowed all thoughts of being gay. Instead, she'd lope over to pump gas while Willa stayed under the tree with Clover and tried to teach the dog to hear by alternately whispering and shouting in her ear. After a while, she let Willa take Clover for walks in the empty fields behind the gas station. She'd hear the portable radio, when the wind was right, going farther away and coming back again.

During those times, the hole Regina had left

closed up and Andy started looking for a place of her own, dreaming of settling down forever, of taking what she'd been given, this peace among these kind people, of losing this melancholy that had settled even in her muscles. It helped to take pictures of the tree, the gas station, Willa in her light blue uniform in front of her cleaning cart at the motel. This was her real life now.

Andy started driving Willa home when she got off work, to save Mrs. Kohl coming by. She'd stay to supper, and Willa's father, an English teacher at the high school, would hold court. She understood why the women did all their talking away from home.

"I'm a disappointed man, Andrea," said Mr. Kohl, still in a tie at the dinner table. "I named each of these children for Midwestern writers: Willa Cather Kohl, Booth Tarkington Kohl, Theodore Dreiser Kohl, and only Ernest Hemingway chose to go to college. Even he's only studying farming."

"I guess you used up all the brains in the family, Daddy," said Willa, rolling her eyes at Andy. She'd confided under the tree one day that they were all smart enough, just didn't want to be like their stuffy dad.

"We'll see what the grandchildren do," answered Mr. Kohl, like his lines were memorized. "Maybe this generation is just a fallow field and the next yield will be richer." He puffed on his pipe.

Mr. Kohl deserved a punch in the mouth, Andy felt. She was protective toward her new friend, even though she'd just walked away without a fight when her own dad had dismissed her.

Willa explained, "You have to take him with a grain of salt. He's just a snob. I don't get all the reading he does. Did you see how thick his glasses were? I use my eyes for knitting and I'll have something in the end." She looked at Andy's almost gangly body. "How'd you like a sweater for the winter? I'll bet you look like a million dollars in red."

That was the moment Andy started wanting to dance with Willa Kohl.

CHAPTER TEN

She knew she'd never forget the night she and Willa sat atop the double ferris wheel and stared right into the mouth of the full moon.

They were so close to it they played at being able to see all its features. "Looks like it's getting ready to gobble us up," Willa said, her voice trembling with the fear and excitement of another descent.

Again and again they flew to the top just long enough to get an eyeful of the moon and sweep back down. Andy was having so much fun that she'd been forgetting Regina off and on all night. It scared her, that surrender of vigilance, of her resolve to concentrate on reaching Regina before it was too late. At the same time she felt a guilty relief to lose the pain for a while.

"Are you shaking?" asked Willa.

In answer, Andy held up her hand. It trembled against the blue night, the yellow-orange moon, the neon lights of the rides.

"You're not scared of the ferris wheel, are you, Andy?"

She shook her head no, remembering the roller coaster Frenchy had taken them on at Coney Island. She wanted to lay her trembling hand on Willa's bare arm. It looked soft, like her comforter, and the dark hairs that lay across it stood in the chilly breeze. She let her eyes close as she turned her head away and felt the next fall without seeing it. Music from all the rides clashed below them and barkers challenged the strolling crowds.

She kept her hand to herself, but Willa reached to hold it.

"What are you scared of, then, Andy?"

They went up again. "Maybe nothing." She would *not* kiss Willa; she was *not* going to be gay with her. She breathed deeply the exciting smells of popcorn and cotton candy. When she opened her eyes, Willa's hand lay against the arm of her good white shirt, the same shirt Regina had unbuttoned so slowly night after night. The thought of Regina came as a shock again, but Willa's touch diluted the pain.

After a final amazing swoop when the top wheel

switched to the bottom wheel, and the bottom stopped abruptly before a harassed attendant, they walked down the ramp to Willa's family.

"How was it?" asked Mrs. Kohl, who would go on no rides, but now ate her second cotton candy.

While Willa described the ferris wheel with rapture, Andy got pictures of the group. She remembered some snapshots from her childhood, taken by one of the rides at Weirs Beach — Ma in a bouffant hairdo, Gramma with that suspicious look she always gave cameras, and Andy in the cowboy hat she'd worn everywhere that summer, the strap under her chin fastened with a wooden bead that pinched her neck. She snapped another picture now, feeling as safe inside this new family circle as she had back then.

She was certain, though, that the Kohls would be furious if they knew of her temptation. They liked and trusted her, had no idea what she'd done with Regina. They probably thought gay people were as bad as the Ayatollah had been. She wouldn't betray their trust.

Willa innocently took her arm as they passed through the crowd, and applauded as Andy played the carnival games with the Kohl brothers. When she finally won a soft tiny green plaid dog, she turned to give it to Mrs. Kohl, but Willa's eyes were so expectant that Andy presented it to her instead. Willa hugged it, then hugged Andy right there in front of the family. Maybe you didn't have to be queer to win something for another woman in this part of the country.

The next afternoon, wet air hung heavily over the gas station. Andy worked in it sluggishly; it had all the substance of her gloom. Thunder rolled across faraway cornfields, lightning teased the sky. Now and then a chilly bit of breeze exploded on her skin and she felt like everything was about to break.

A half hour later it broke overhead, just as Willa crossed the lot to her.

"Whew!" said Willa, leaping out of reach of the splashing raindrops. "What a day. The weather's pulling in so many people from the road I'm about worked to death. It must be quitting time for you."

"I can drive you home," Andy offered.

"Come on back over to the motel then. I'll get my purse."

Andy finished up and drove the Studebaker next door. Just those few minutes of drenching rain and lightning-rent sky convinced her that she had no business trying to make it back into town till the storm let up.

"We can wait it out in here!" Willa yelled from an open doorway.

Andy and Clover dashed through the downpour, but were soaked by the time they reached the motel. Willa was in a room that needed plumbing repairs and couldn't be rented. The curtains were closed. Andy noticed that Willa had switched on the lamp beside the double bed as well as her portable radio. The room quickly took on a homey wet dog smell.

"No, Clover!" Andy uselessly commanded when the dog jumped on the bed. She led her as far from it as she could, and stood awkwardly beside the panting dog, realizing what it meant to be alone in a motel room with a woman. With Willa. After fighting Regina tooth and nail about motels all the way to Ohio, here she was.

71

"You're drenched!" cried Willa, coming at her with a towel.

She struggled, but Willa soon had her on the bed and was vigorously rubbing her head. Andy could see that Willa wasn't much drier. Her uniform outlined the hardened nipples of her heavy breasts.

Willa toweled her own hair then, tossing her barrettes to the dresser. When she took the towel away, Willa was transformed. Normally, the barrettes pulled her hair tightly back from her big white face. Now it fell like thick, wavy drapery, and her face took on shadows and curves. Willa looked up at her from under her eyelashes, then unbuttoned and slipped out of the top half of her uniform and bra before Andy could stop her.

Andy backed away. She stared at Willa, trying not to.

"Didn't you ever see a naked woman before, Andy?"

"Sure I did."

"We're both girls, you know."

"I know," she said. Her voice sounded like a croak. She grabbed the towel and knelt to Clover, throwing all her energy into drying the dog.

Willa laughed from the edge of the bed where she brushed that cloud-like hair. The lamplight made it shine. "Your hair's standing straight up," she told Andy. "Come here and let me fix it."

Andy couldn't take a step forward. Willa moved to her instead. She smelled like the comforter from the thrift store. Mrs. Kohl must launder the donations at home in the same detergent she used for her family, thought Andy. Willa turned Andy around, very matter-of-factly, and brushed her hair until it lay flat.

But when Andy stepped away, Willa pulled her back by her garage jacket. "How come you still have this wet thing on?" And she yanked and pulled until Andy stood there in her rolled up red sleeves, goosebumps on her arms.

There were free postcards on the dresser. Desperately Andy focused on them, and thought of her family. She'd sent a couple cards to her folks from Indiana, but hadn't called since she left Ohio. Andy sat in the only chair, but what could she do with her eyes? Willa was back on the edge of the bed again, brushing and brushing, her breasts lifting with each stroke.

"Andy, why don't you come over here?"

It would be worse to have to explain why she wouldn't sit with her. She went to the spot Willa patted.

Willa lay her hand on Andy's arm in the same way she had on the ferris wheel the night before. There was that falling-out-of-the-sky feeling again. There was the woman, half naked, next to her, breasts lovelier than was bearable.

"How come you never talk about the friend you traveled with?"

She shrugged, feeling annoyed. How could she? Willa would guess that she was gay. Even when she was a little kid people looked at her funny on the street. One day in the dentist's waiting room another girl asked, "Why's that boy wearing a dress, Mommy?" Andy's mom never seemed to notice these things. She'd just keep fussing with the newest baby.

"Tell me about her," Willa said. "Were you close? Did you stay in motels together?"

"She was okay," she answered gruffly, not meeting Willa's eyes.

Poor Willa was just trying to be nice, Andy thought. Willa couldn't know how suffocated she felt holding it in. All she wanted to do was push Willa down and lay beside her, maybe kiss those soft breasts a while. Then she could talk. She swallowed when Willa lay back, her breasts flattening and cascading down her sides.

"Why did you leave her behind? Did you fight?"

"No." She dared another look at Willa. "She just wasn't a nice woman like you."

Willa looked exasperated. "But Andy, you've been so many places and met so many people. I'm stuck here. I wish you'd tell me about the world, about your friend. Was she mean to you?"

"Kind of." Andy turned away. "Maybe your shirt is dry."

She thought Willa was reaching for it, but instead felt Willa's arms around her from the back.

"Andy, Andy, do you think I'd be mean to you too?"

Andy stayed stock still. Could she reach Clover with her foot, to wake her? The dog would probably jump all over them and get her out of this.

But oh, the soft, white womanly body, the sweet smell of talcum and shampoo, the little heart beating against her back. She moved away and sat on the bed, clutching the bedspread to keep her hands to herself.

"Do you think I'm awful?" Willa asked, sitting beside her and leaning her head on Andy's shoulder.

74

Andy couldn't help it. Her arm reached around Willa to hold her.

"No."

"Then what are you scared of?"

"You're too nice."

Willa went silent a while. "Is that why your friend *wasn't* nice?"

"Sometimes she was."

"I would always be nice to you. I love you, Andy."

She had to look at Willa then, at the love shining in her eyes, at the wanting swell of her mouth. What about the peaceful life she was building?

Willa caressed her hand, kissing it all over.

Andy pulled it away. "I can't *think!*"

"Then *don't* think!"

"What if they find out?"

"This is nineteen eighty-nine, Andy. Gay people are on the news all the time. Even the shows have gay characters. They can't do anything to us any more."

Could she be right?

"Even if they could, I don't give a hoot," Willa said, her face red and determined. "It's my life and I'll live it like I want. It's *you* I love, not some farmer no better than a bull."

"But what kind of life would it be for you, everybody hating you?"

"It's just strangers they hate. I'm from here and they know I'm not going to hurt anyone."

"It's better just to be friends. You're asking for trouble otherwise."

"Then come here, trouble," Willa challenged with

a crook of her finger. It was as if flirtatious, teasing Regina suddenly inhabited Willa's body. Andy threw herself face down on the bed.

"Andy, Andy," soothed Willa, running a hand along her back, slipping it under her overalls, then as far as the beginning of the crack in Andy's bottom.

It was too much for Andy. She rolled over and pulled Willa down, kissing her.

"Willa," she said, breaking away again, "you don't understand."

"Maybe I don't, honeybun, but I can." Willa kissed her then, pressing her whole body into Andy's, rubbing herself against her, kissing her with her tongue. Andy liked it too much to stop and kissed her back, letting their tongues push, play, feeling the soft flesh of Willa everywhere with her hands. She rolled on top of Willa.

How could she feel like this again? Her breath got faster and faster and she was sweating. Her whole body felt like it was wrapped in a blood pressure tester, ready to burst with lust and a raging need to be loving someone. Willa's legs opened under her, her hips pushed at Andy.

"I've been waiting for you so long," Willa said, her hands tearing the shirt from Andy's pants.

Just then came a pounding on the door.

They froze. Clover was still asleep at the foot of the bed. Andy found herself listening for a sound outside the door so intently that her ears hurt. All she could think of was that Roy had found them.

But this wasn't Regina she was squirming away from.

"Who's there?" called Willa. Her voice was calm, but her eyes were wide and staring.

Andy hadn't locked the door. It opened and there stood Kerwin from the gas station, yellow slicker dripping, talking through his nose. In his thirties, married, he'd been nasty to her from the start. The owner had given some of Kerwin's hours to her because Kerwin was such a poor worker.

"Sorry to interrupt you, *ladies*," he said with the sneer he used on customers. She followed his eyes to Willa, who held Andy's jacket in front of her breasts.

"The boss just called to say he couldn't make it back because of the storm and could you stay a while. I told him I saw you come over here."

"Sure," said Andy as if she had nothing better to do. She didn't dare look back as she left, hands in pockets, whistling, with Kerwin.

As the summer wore on, the weather was either too hot to live with, or it rained and thundered without restraint. Every time they got into a motel room, they'd indulge in long bouts of making out in front of the soap operas. She always felt guilty, for indulging her own passions, for being with someone besides Regina, for being so weak-willed about fighting this gay thing. Sometimes she wanted to leave town and put it all behind her, sometimes she believed Willa that it would be okay.

"Did you ever see a tornado, Andy?" Willa asked one day.

"No."

"They can do a lot of damage. The weatherman keeps saying we're bound to get one."

Andy was opening the drapes, looking toward the gas station.

"What're you thinking about, honeybun?" asked Willa at the next commercial.

"Kerwin."

"Is he coming up here again?"

"No, but he's always watching me."

"Oh, don't worry about him. Everyone knows he's a lamebrain. Mad at the world. And he smells awful, like canned peas."

They laughed, but Andy felt like the weatherman, certain of tornadoes. She could smell Roy in the air.

The gas station owner came early one day and asked Kerwin to watch the pumps. He took Andy inside and swiveled toward her on the old cracked office chair.

"How are you doing, Andy?" he asked.

"All right." She was suspicious. He hadn't brought her in here to ask about her health, that was for sure.

"What do you think about this Pete Rose gambling thing? Looks like even baseball's not sacred anymore, is it?"

The room stank from decades of cigarette smoke. Her knees shook and she had to go to the bathroom. She knew this was the end again even if she'd been honorable with Willa and not gone all the way. What would she do if Indiana didn't work out for her? She was sweating with fear. Where could she go next?

"I hear you've been spending time in a motel room over there with that high school teacher's daughter."

She watched his face without a word, hiding the terror she felt blossom inside her like an atom bomb.

"What do you do in there?"

She was tempted to scowl at him and walk away, but he'd been so good to her up till now. "Watch the soap operas."

"Well, it doesn't look right, Andy. I don't think you ought to go over there any more. Let the girl watch her shows at home."

She went out to pump gas. Kerwin whistled like a regular fool and winked at every man who came into the station. One minute she was flushed mad at him for making trouble, wanting to tear him into shreds, the next agreeing with the owner that motel rooms were no place for nice girls. She'd stop it with Willa.

"They have no right to snoop into our business!" cried Willa when Andy told her what had happened. "You stop this Studebaker. I'm going back there to give them what for, that owner who cheats on his wife and the whole town knows it, and old Kerwin the canned pea."

"We'd only lose our jobs."

"You can't just let them push you around like that, Andy Blaine. Let me out of the car this minute!"

She had to admire the woman. Clover jumped into the front seat. Andy watched in the rearview mirror as Willa marched back to the station. She didn't want any part of it. Willa would find out the hard way what the world thought of women like them. She'd been low before, but now depression set in so deep her head felt heavy.

The next morning she was cleaning out the Reverend's roof gutters when the old Chevy pulled up. The gas station owner walked across the lawn she'd preened to a uniform green.

He squinted up at her. "I have to let you go, Andy."

She stared at him. He handed her a last paycheck, with two weeks' severance pay in it. Her work glove, smelling like moderling leaves, was making it filthy.

"You're a darn good worker and I wish you well, but we just don't allow anything like that in Lebanon," he told her. "Take this and go to San Francisco or Minneapolis where you can get away with it."

She watched his car drive down the road. Should she start packing now? Should she go by the motel and tell Willa? Quit the Reverend before he found out?

Just like Gramma always said, she was a true Thursday's child, and "Thursday's Child has far to go."

It was too late to quit the Reverend. The phone rang in the house before she'd gotten halfway around the roof. Was she any better than this muck in the gutters? She looked at it against her work glove. There wasn't a thing wrong with dead leaves and dirt. They were perfectly natural. Wasn't she? Why was this happening to her? Maybe it was past time to chase after Regina again. Or maybe this was all her fault for not staying completely away from women.

By the time the Reverend came out of his house she felt sadder than a sky about to rain. She didn't know how to be gay and she didn't know how not to be gay. She tensed as if he would hit her.

"Stop working for a minute, Andy." She looked out toward the horizon. "I guess you know why I'm here," he said with sympathy in his voice. "But I want you to know I don't condemn you."

She felt a stream of hope like sunshine enter her heart.

"I've been back East to study and I know very well this is the twentieth century. I know there are people like you and that you suffer for something you can't help. I don't believe in punishing you for your nature."

It was strange to hear him say the same thing Frenchy had. Would she have to give in and be gay?

"Still," the Reverend went on, "I think you might be happier in a big city like Chicago. Around here you could get hurt, and no one will hire you now."

"We just fooled around, sir," she told him. Her gloves had gotten damp through and she wanted to take them off, but exposing the hands that had touched Regina and Willa didn't feel safe. "We didn't do anything like we could have."

"That isn't the way Willa Kohl tells it. She claims she's found out with you that she's a lesbian and she's going to marry you any way she can."

She sighed long and deep. Poor Willa. Her

parents knew, then. What did the Kohls
think of her now? They'd been so nice and here
she'd gone and"

"I correspond with a minister in Chicago who
works with a lot of gay people. I'm certain Reverend
Brandeis will know who to call for help. Here's his
address. It would probably be best to leave this
afternoon to avoid any further unpleasantness. I
think I can come up with some funds to make your
move easier."

Everything in her screamed *No!* She hadn't
exactly been happy here, but Willa was a good
woman and believed in the safety of the place.
Couldn't they prove their worth somehow? Couldn't
she fight to stay?

Whether she stayed or went, she'd have to move
out of the church garage. After Reverend Carrier
went inside she climbed off the ladder and hugged
Clover.

"You love me no matter what, don't you, dog?"
she asked. Clover didn't hesitate to lick every bit of
her face with her rough cool slimy tongue. The
whole world smelled like Milk-Bones.

She packed everything she owned into that old
Studebaker — her comforter, her plates, her tin box
full of food, her good shirt, the little stereo, her
dad's gas station jacket and her camera. She hefted
Clover's food in, and filled a jug of water for the
road. At least she had money this time. She'd cash
her checks on the way out of town no matter how
people looked at her.

When she got to the motel, Willa was wheeling
her cart between rooms. "What are you doing here?"

Willa asked. Her eyes looked red, her face more pale than usual.

"I'm getting run out of town."

"The bastards," Willa hissed. "Come in our room and talk. We'll find a way around this one, Andy. You can't leave me."

"No. The motel room got us in enough trouble."

"Andy, don't be silly. What do you think they'd do, kill you?"

"Maybe," she answered with all seriousness. "Even if they didn't, the Reverend fired me, the gas station fired me, I can't get work around here now."

"I'd support us both. Where would you go?"

"The Reverend says there's more people like me up in Chicago."

"Then I'll come with you." Willa untied her apron.

Another trip with another woman? Where would this one end? Did Willa really know what she wanted, or did she, like Regina, just want a ride out of town? How could she ever stop being gay with Willa along? "You come on when I get settled if you want. I'm not fit to be with right now."

"What if they run *me* out of town? I don't even have a car."

"You have family here. You told me they wouldn't dare. Besides, you can tell them it's all my fault. I came here and made you do it."

Tears filled Willa's eyes. "You mean you don't want me."

She looked at Willa. It was true. She didn't want another burden. Her own self was heavy enough. "You take your time deciding, then we'll talk. Here's

83

the Chicago minister I'm going to see. And I'll send you my address."

"No, Andy. I love you. Life can't ever be the same here for me." The tears came then.

"It's not doing you any good to be seen here with me now. I'd better go." She put Clover in the car.

"Wait! I have something for you."

Willa ran off to the laundry room and came back with an enormous red sweater. "I finished this last night, while my father was browbeating me. I needed something to keep me from going crazy."

"It's beautiful," said Andy.

"Put it on, quick. I want to see you in it."

She did, despite the heat.

"You look like fire," Willa told her, tears flowing as if to put the fire out. "Your red hair and that sweater — you're just beautiful, Andy. I can't let you go." Willa grabbed her and hugged her hard. "What am I going to do?" she wailed.

"I guess I'm lucky. I've been different all my life, one way or the other. That makes it a little bit easier when everybody treats you like a murderer."

"You're so good, Andy. How can they take you away from me?" Willa stood back from her. "I'm not going to change my mind," she said, her face going hard. "I'm gay too. I'll always be. Even if I stay here I'll never marry some man. And I'm not going to stay here. If you won't take me to Chicago, I'll go to New York City and find your friend Frenchy Tonneau. You'll see," she vowed, hurling her apron onto the cart.

Andy surveyed the landscape. No, she couldn't stay where no one but Willa wanted her, and besides, Willa was better off without her. She imagined the rearview mirror. The cornfield would narrow behind her, more and more, until Willa, a small figure in the road, disappeared altogether, along with the motel, the gas station and the whole little town.

Clover was already in the Studebaker, sitting up tall, whining, raring to go, paw on the steering wheel. Willa stood in the road, face buried in her hands, crying. Andy had a sudden memory of Regina at the race. One minute she'd been on the sidelines letting Roy decide her fate, the next she'd leapt in the car. Would Willa leap in too? Not if she knew what was good for her.

CHAPTER ELEVEN

Andy had her first clear view of Lake Michigan from Route 90 going north to Chicago. She got off to see more of the city and found herself on Chicago's South Side. The further she drove the more disoriented she became. Her head felt like one of the little animals struck dead on the side of the road. She kept smiling apologetically at the black people she passed because she didn't belong in their territory.

"I never asked to be gay," she groaned. Life had been just fine before love came along.

"I had a Studebaker," she told Clover as she looked for signs north, "and a nice job at the auto body shop. After high school, I cleaned up those two rooms over Dad's garage and I stayed there for the next three years. You would've liked it, kid," she said, mussing the dog's fur. "I wasn't far from the arcades down at the beach, and you could have come out on the lake with me and Everett and John. You'd like John. He's into animals and nature. Everett laughs at him for throwing his fish back." She groaned again, feeling bruised from head to toe. "What in heck are we doing in Chicago?"

Her eyes hurt terribly, like they did when she had the flu. She'd been ignoring these growing aches since morning, but now they raged. By the time she reached Lake Shore Drive her chest hurt so badly she could hardly steer. "What am I going to do?" The fear was coming in big explosions now. Her heart raced. She had no one here. Didn't even know a doctor if she was sick. Worst of all, she kept mistaking women on the street for Regina. There was another one. Was this some kind of punishment for being gay? Her hands shook. She wanted to cry out for help.

She forced the Studebaker through rush hour, letting the traffic guide her. The minister lived on Devon Street, way north of where she was. Now and then she glanced toward the lake. It was a big one, all right.

She should turn right around and go home. Ma would put her to bed. She could almost hear her pesky brothers running wild on the packed dirt yard the way they had when they were little. Her dad had been in the Army repairing trucks and heavy

87

equipment in Vietnam, so there were seven years before Everett and John followed like marching soldiers one right after the other. Gramma was supposed to help bring the boys up, but she'd died just after John was born. Ma was focused on the baby, so Andy kind of lost Ma at the same time that she lost Gramma.

Right at this minute some clean sheets and a noisy household sounded a lot better than talking to a minister, than feeling like a bruised thumb right after a hammer hit it, than going on when she needed to stop.

When I was sick and lay-a-bed, she remembered Gramma reciting. What was the rest of it? *I had two pillows by my head, And all my toys beside me lay* — She'd known it by heart once. *To keep me happy all the day.*

Then she remembered. Everybody from work, and all their friends, all the kids she'd gone to school with, knew she was gay. She couldn't go home.

She came to a red light, but felt even worse. She wished she could drive on forever. The Studebaker seemed to hum the old poem underneath her, around her. She opened a window because the smell of canned peas pervaded the car.

How could Chicago have so many people who looked like Regina? She saw her hurry off a bus, out of an elevated train station, saw her rush into a supermarket called Treasure Island, carry a basket out of a laundromat, stroll into an apartment building.

Andy pulled into the no-parking zone in front of the church. Would she always be waiting outside somewhere now, wanting help? Would she ever be able to take care of herself out in the world? It seemed impossible. She hadn't the strength to get out of the car. Her ears were hot, drawing breath was like breathing fire. She lay against Clover's side staring at the ticking clock, scared, and hoped someone would take care of her dog because she couldn't.

The next few hours happened in a fog. When she woke up on a couch she thought at first she was back in Weirs Beach because all she could see from her burning eyes was one of those old-fashioned metal-topped kitchen tables like her folks had. Her eyes shut and she reached for her toys. Her insides felt like an elevator shaft, her heart like a cableless elevator falling, falling. Where were her toys? "Ma!" she shouted, but heard nothing. Was this a dream? Was this hell? When she opened her eyes again she saw the table, red on white, chips and scratches Everett and John had put there. She tried to lift her head to see better, but it felt so full of darkness, and so heavy, she gave up. She lay there smelling canned peas.

A while later she became aware of clean white sheets. They were soft from washing, and darned, like the sheets she and Regina had bought from the Goodwill store in Columbus. Her ponderous heart clenched with fear. She was still gay then, and this fear and illness would never end. Every time she moved the elevator fell. She shook with fear and whimpered like a baby, "Help me, help me."

Two men were talking. One voice was high-pitched, the other just a mumble. She smiled. Willa's brothers, of course! The thought was so comforting that she didn't open her eyes again until sunlight covered her. No, those weren't Willa's brothers. Gradually she remembered Reverend Brandeis and two other men easing her into the back of her car. She'd lain shivering next to Clover. Fear clamped her muscles again.

"Clover?" she asked, her voice so hoarse she barely recognized it. Her throat felt like she'd swallowed a rasp.

"You awake, wanderer?" the high-pitched voice called. He sounded like one of Frenchy's friends.

"Clover?" she was able to repeat.

One of the men rose. When he stood next to the couch where she lay, she had to make sure she wasn't dreaming. Slight, he had a huge puff of frizzy hair, redder than her own, all around his face. He wore a robe of a polished dark blue material dotted with crescent moons, stars, and planets with rings around them. His red beard was so thick it pointed like a third arm toward her. He looked something like the wizard in *Fantasia,* but his smile was like an angel's. Had she really made it into heaven, not hell after all? Maybe she'd been beamed to another planet filled with wizards and Reginas.

"I'm Starr," he said, laying his hand on her forehead. He spoke quickly, as if he had to pack a great deal into every sentence or be silent forever. "Reverend Brandeis called us to help you. Is Clover your dog? She's out back, in the little fenced-in patch of a garden we have."

"The garden's his pride and joy," added the other man, softly, from the table. "We told her not to dig."

"She's deaf."

"Your dog? It's a good thing Kyle's a signer." The wizard laughed softly.

90

She didn't know what signing was, but she saw the way Starr looked at Kyle. She knew well enough what love looked like. She ached to be looked at like that again.

"That old Studebaker of yours is locked up in the garage. *We* don't have anything to park in there," said Kyle. He moved to the couch. "How're you feeling, hon?"

"Nasty," she answered. Her ears were so clogged her voice sounded far away. "But I'll be okay. I have money for an apartment."

"Oh, hush," admonished Starr. "We keep our home open to gay brothers and sisters in need. Want some tea?" Didn't he ever breathe when he talked?

"But I'm not gay any more," she said and she cried herself to sleep.

Later, she woke from a dream that a man was undressing her. She opened her eyes. It was night again and Kyle really was undressing her. Terrified, she pushed him away. "I'm not straight either," her voice rasped.

"It's okay, Andy, I'm a registered nurse. I do this all the time." Kyle had a slow brutal look to him, like a reformed bully. His gentle touch felt like leashed strength, but his careful eyes and kind smile told her she had nothing to fear. She relaxed.

"Roy was in my dream. All the kids back home. They were watching the race," she told Kyle, as if he'd been there. "The more they watched, and cheered Roy on, the sicker I got. And Regina's boss, he was there. He looked at me and I started to burn up. Verne put her arms around me and crushed me till my chest felt like, like it does right now. Am I going crazy or dying?"

Kyle dressed her in a pair of Starr's pajamas, then held and rocked her, cooing at her like her mother had done to the little babies. His hair was in a buzz cut and he wore thick blue-tinted glasses. Deep lines drooped from either side of his nose like a handlebar moustache. He looked middle-aged. Above his barrel chest and thick neck his eyes were a soothing green. "You have a very low fever, just barely above normal. Reverend Brandeis told us what happened in Indiana. That kind of treatment would make me feel crazy too. You're going to be all right." When she was calmer he settled her back on the couch.

She closed her eyes and lay back on pine needles in the woods. She gazed up into the green, green of the trees, her fear gone.

It came back, though, and during the next weeks she was certain she'd never see trees again, would never get off that couch. She went to a clinic. The doctor talked about stress and anxiety and prescribed more rest. In the night she lay awake taking the deep breaths Starr prescribed, but every inhalation burned her with dread. Starr's endless talk merged with Gramma's nursery rhymes and country/western music into a weird, high-pitched whirring. She felt as if she had her headset on, tuned to static.

But little by little, she began to catch rays of light in her life. Kyle and Starr supplied some of them.

"Don't give me that look," Starr said one day as he changed the paper over the lamp shade to green. "Color therapy works. It's one reason I'm alive." He lowered his voice. "I have a perfectly worthless heart. It's so bad, Social Security gives me money to stay home, keep house for Kyle and minister to my little flock. But herbs, light, music, yoga — I'm still here! And you will be too. We'll bathe you in green light till you're healthy."

"Is it AIDS?" she asked in a small voice, filled with apprehension.

Starr looked at her so long she thought he was trying to say yes. "You're for real," he finally answered. "You don't know a thing about it do you?" He explained about HIV.

Two days later sun streamed into the kitchen window, making Starr's hair glow. He was baking bread and cooking something that smelled spicy in a big pot. She broke out into a sweat of anxiety. She could smell something besides canned peas again! Did that mean she was rejoining the living, that she'd have to take up her old burdens?

"No!" she cried and retreated back to her couch where she didn't have to be gay.

CHAPTER TWELVE

The leaves fell off the trees during her autumn in Chicago, but they lacked the fiery New England glory. As her symptoms disappeared one by one, leaving only a great weakness and weepiness, she spent hours sitting in the afternoon sun on the front stoop watching the neighbors pass by.

She took pictures of them: the kerchiefed old woman with an accent so thick Andy never understood a word she said, the professional dog walker with two leashes in one hand and three in the other who looked like a water witch on a hot but erratic trail. The sharp click of her camera was a safe way to be part of life again. She could look at people from behind a lens.

Her paychecks were half gone, and she might be able to handle a part-time job, but the thought of looking for work gave her a major case of the dreads. She called her ma and asked her to withdraw all the money she'd saved working since high school.

When the papergirl delivered, Andy would glance at the headlines, but for the most part they were more than she could handle. Murder, war, overpopulation, hunger, rape, gay-bashing, a huge earthquake in California. She took it all personally, as if she were the world itself.

As the days grew chillier, she unpacked the red sweater Willa had knit her. She wore it while sitting on the front stoop, trying not to feel too much too soon. She still hadn't sent her address to Willa. At first it was because she was so sick. Now she didn't want to. Willa was better off, she thought bitterly, without trying to be gay.

Nights, she'd sit around the apartment with Starr and Kyle, listening to their music, their talk, to the friends who stopped by, mostly from Starr's little church. Services were held Sunday morning in the artist's big loft space upstairs. There were always at least half a dozen men there, often a sprinkling of shy women in couples.

"I've threatened to name it the Temple of the Stray Redeemer," Starr said, "but Kyle claims the congregation would think they needed green stamps to pray. You know, for one thousand stamps you can be forgiven for your sins?"

The gatherings were warm, bright, homey. She loved the people who came and when it was time to move around the room to say hello and hug she joined in, grateful as she'd never thought she could be for the touching, crying at every smile.

She loved, too, to listen to the nighttime visitors tell their stories. As they talked in the lamplit living room about how they'd made their way to Chicago and to the church, she realized they weren't so different from her. One was from the Washington coast, another from Louisville, yet another from the Florida Keys. They'd followed love, every one of them, and ended up without it, then found it, lost it again and often again.

One night Starr told his story, speaking as fast and breathlessly as ever. As usual, he seemed to love being the center of attention. He'd studied for years to be a rabbi. Like Andy, he hadn't known he was gay until he fell for a man.

"I followed him to San Francisco, but he got tired of me. I moved back to Brooklyn, but my father didn't want me by then either. My mother slipped me enough money to pay rent on a cheap walkup in the East Village. My closest friends and neighbors were cockroaches, but I'd broken away from home, from the Yeshiva, and I was doing what I wanted for the first time in my life. I was living as a woman. I joined S.T.A.R., the radical transvestite group, and named myself after them. My real name is Stan. It felt utterly right to devote my life to loving and comforting men."

He'd risen to pour tea and settled again on the huge velour cushions he'd made for the apartment.

"My father found me then. I watched how heartbroken he was that I'd rejected my maleness, and I began to wonder. Could I, with the woman-hating that I'd been bred to, fulfill myself living as a woman? I went through a stage of begging him for money to change my sex, but he refused and I had, praise be, no other way to fund the operation. It took a long time for me to realize that I only needed to let the female side of me live, not to kill the male in me. I didn't need phony breasts to do that."

Andy sometimes thought Starr acted like he was in a hippie soap opera, but, like her, he was different from other people, so she tried to love him that much more.

"It was the hardest decision I ever made, against transsexualism, against transvestitism. I was dropping the trappings of the last identifiable groups I could ever belong to. I was choosing to live as something so abhorrent it didn't even have a name. Was I a radical feminist? A revolutionary? A faggot? An aberration among aberrations?"

Another night it was Kyle who spoke. "When I was married, my wife —"

"You were *married?*" asked Andy.

"Does that shock you?"

"I didn't know gay people ever got married."

Kyle laughed his dry, almost silent laugh. "I was so damned straight I was thrilled to get my first tie, play my first high school football game, go out on my first date with a girl." Starr rubbed Kyle's crewcut.

She could see Kyle in a football uniform, grease

under his eyes, plowing down his opponents with a ball under his burly arm. Once or twice she'd feared for Starr, watching Kyle's temper flare, his fists curl.

"I went to the right college, played every sport, thought doing it with a teammate made me one of the boys. The day I married I signed the partnership papers to go into Dad's car dealership. Only the family didn't really approve of my wife. She was intelligent, handsome, and different. More like a pal. Later I saw that I wanted to *be* her, not be married to her. And sex? Oh, girlfriend. Put a fag and a dyke together and watch the disaster you can get. She came out to me the day I came out to her."

Clover paced restlessly at the front door. Andy didn't want to miss a word. She'd always liked history, but there hadn't been any place in it for her before, she thought as she pulled on her red sweater. The fall air was crisp and dark. She could hear the traffic throb out on Devon, puffing exhaust. She was tired and sat on the back steps while Clover sought newer smells along the alleyway.

She thought of the group upstairs. It seemed like she wasn't the only one who'd had a hard time starting out gay. Was she being chicken to try and back out now? Could she? Look at me, she thought, living with gays, going to church with gays, hanging out with them.

A car's brakes screeched on the side street at the end of the alley. Where was Clover? Her body leapt down the steps and she ran at full speed like the old Andy.

Clover sauntered up the alleyway toward her, an oblivious smile across her muzzle, and finished what she had to do. The car roared away into the heedless city.

"You horse's ass," she said, hugging Clover.

Legs shaking from her sprint, she peered through the window at that old Studebaker. She hadn't really looked at it since she'd arrived. Even the thought of it gave her that quavery feeling, like she'd panic and get sick again. But there it sat, quietly gleaming, reflecting the light from someone's apartment. Someday she'd get in it again. The thought brought back her nausea, but she supposed she and Clover couldn't stay here forever.

When Andy returned, still damp and chilled from Clover's close call, a woman about her age had joined the circle. Clover bounded to her as if they were old friends. The woman, tall, spare, had skin that seemed too dark for freckles, yet there they were, dancing across her nose, leaping onto round, high cheekbones.

The woman rose and held out a long-fingered hand. "I'm Mandy Tolliver." Her smile was wide, loose and glad-looking, her voice on the low side. Andy remembered seeing her in church.

"Mandy's a musician. A sax player," said Kyle.

The woman bobbed her head and bent her knees, pretending to play. "Just call me Tolliver so we don't sound like Mutt and Jeff: Mandy and Andy."

"I'm a Southerner too," Tolliver told the man from Key West in an accent that sounded like syrup. "New Orleans is my home turf, but there's no work there for someone like me. I'm no Banu Gibson, no Queen Ida, no Pete Fountain. I don't fit the mold. I can always get a gig in some little club here without

99

being a name. Chicago suits me better, except for the damned cold."

"The rest of us followed lovers here," offered Louisville.

"You think that old saxophone isn't my lover? Shit, it keeps me company when women get nasty."

"Are you still seeing Ruby?" Starr asked.

"In my dreams, you mean?" She shook her head, face resigned. "We, like, just can't seem to work it out, except in the music. Ruby sings at a piano bar," she told Andy. "Once in a while with me. She's got hair the color of autumn leaves in sunshine, and eyes as green as a New Orleans lagoon.,"

"Her voice isn't bad either," Kyle added, a laugh in his gruff voice.

Straining forward, Andy tried to make out every word. She'd never known a musician before, or a Southerner, or for that matter, a black person. Tolliver was exotic to her, a whole other way of being gay, and yet she had her problems with women too.

Tolliver kept coming back to hear Starr's Paul Winter tapes. She talked with Andy and invited her to visit. Andy was petrified and threw up all morning before she left, but Starr talked her out the door, promising to take care of Clover. Shakily, not at all sure she was ready to reenter life, she walked over to Ashland Street where Ruby and Tolliver lived.

"Come on in," Tolliver said, "I'll show you around the collective."

Andy's knees were quivering again. She nestled her freezing hands in her overall pockets. She wanted to run from these new people, new lesbians.

But the house smelled like unchanged kitty litter and garlic, looked shabby and comforting. "What *is* a collective?"

Tolliver led her to the kitchen. "See this chart? It's a list of chores and whose turn it is to do what when. Everybody shares the work. Then, like we have house meetings every week to discuss what to do about the ones who slack off."

Andy looked at the chart, which seemed too confusing to read, and then at Tolliver.

"It doesn't make much sense to me, either," Tolliver said, her laughter filling the kitchen. "But the place is cheap, and all lesbian, so I make do. Come on upstairs."

Up tempo piano music shouted from a room somewhere. "That's Ruby," Tolliver whispered. They passed dirty dishes and an overflowing trash can, dust puppies that ambushed them, living room furniture like she'd had in Columbus, and the offending kitty litter pan. These women needed a mother, Andy decided.

Tolliver's room was on the top floor, as tiny as the rest, but clean, if not neat. Andy sat in a deep soft easy chair. Tolliver picked up her saxophone from its stand and slung it from her neck on a strap. Knees apart, she blew into the golden neck and brought out a long low sound that raised the hairs on the back of Andy's neck.

The boys said Mandy Tolliver was good, but Andy had never heard anything like this, even the times she'd gone to weddings. Tolliver's eyes were closed, her lashes long against her high cheekbones. She looked as if she were playing from a source so inside herself she'd never come back. Andy tapped her feet wondering if Tolliver was playing lesbian music.

"Wow," was all she could say when Tolliver set down the instrument.

"Thanks. I like to tell my friends who I am. Saves a lot of useless words. And you, Blaine, I can tell, are a woman of few words." Tolliver looked at her in silence a long moment. "I bet you lost something big, woman."

She shrugged her shoulders. "Just Regina."

"You sound like me. *Just Ruby.* Who's Regina?"

How could she describe Regina, tell the whole tale? She managed, with long pauses and halts, making certain she didn't cry.

Tolliver's head bobbed all the way through. "You did the right thing, leaving Willa behind. But I wouldn't give up on gay if I were you just because of ol' Regina there. I'm getting to the point where I may have to head for the hills too, get away from this Ruby fixation. I know, though, that I can live without her. I'm like you, I just haven't figured out how."

Andy laughed at the rhyme that came to mind. She recited, " *'Tom, Tom, the piper's son,/He learned to play when he was young./But all the tune that he could play/Was 'Over the hills and far away.'* "

"Hey," said Tolliver. "That's cool. Where's that from?" She blew a couple of bars that followed the rhythm of the words.

"Just a nursery rhyme. My Gramma knew them all."

"My daddy was no piper, he was a roustabout on the offshore oil rigs who wouldn't marry Momma. A white man as dark as his oil, never clean. I was glad he didn't live with us. Life would've been easier with some oil money in the bank, but I'm not complaining, I'm where I want to be. You don't have to be, like, rich to blow a horn, thank the Goddess."

"How come you and Starr talk about the Goddess? I mean, is that the same as God?"

"I say Goddess because I relate better to a woman up there. Before I lucked into women's spirituality I thought all that stuff was one big male power trip. I don't really know Starr's trip, but I do know he respects both the masculine and the feminine in people."

Andy smiled. "God always looks like my dad when he's mad."

"No. I think whatever's out there — God, Goddess, the Universe, Divine Energy, whatever it is — loves me a whole lot or I wouldn't have a horn to play, I wouldn't get friends when I need them. You know."

"Don't you have a lot of friends?"

"No. I have a hard time making friends. There's one woman back in New Orleans. An ex-lover."

"I never had many friends. The neighbor kids when I was little. Jeannie from high school."

"Maybe that's why I like you. Two loners. We can be independent cusses together. What do you say?"

"Kind of scary."

"You scared of *me?*"

Her lips were dry. "I've been sick. Life kind of got me down."

"Starr told me. Like a nervous breakdown?"

The words started the anxiety. Tears rushed into her eyes. "Sometimes I just don't know how to live."

"Mega-fear. I can relate."

103

"Why can't you be with Ruby?"

This time Tolliver sighed. "Sex."

"Sex?"

She watched Tolliver, whose head was bowed, her hair red-brown.

"I'm not your Casanova type, like Verne," Tolliver finally answered. "I guess I'm a good enough lover, technically and all that. I certainly get passionate about the women. So I make love to them, but that's like, where it stops."

"Where else would it go?"

"Didn't Regina make love to you too?"

She nodded.

"Well, that's the part I don't do."

"Oh."

"Some women don't mind, they like all the attention. Others, well, they think I don't trust them. They're insulted because they think I'm not letting go."

"Ruby minded?"

"Yes, ma'am."

"Why don't you just give in?"

Tolliver had her arms around herself. "You know, I never talked about this with anyone but a lover before. It's hard. I don't just give in because I can't. I mean, they can work on me all night. It feels good, but I never, you know, come. I want to; I cooperate. It just doesn't happen naturally to me."

"I wonder why you want a woman who doesn't think that's okay."

"You what?" Tolliver asked sharply.

She swallowed her next breath in surprise. Had she angered Tolliver?

"Oh, shit," Tolliver said. Her shoulders heaved as if she were sobbing. The elevator in Andy's stomach plummeted.

After several minutes Tolliver looked up, eyes red. "Shit, Andy, you hit the nail on the head with that one."

"I did?"

"Well, damn it, why *aren't* I with one of those women who don't mind, who're willing to just take. It'd make my life a lot easier. But here I am, wanting — what? Is it Ruby I want, or am I looking for a woman to fix me, a magic lover?" She picked up her sax and put it down again. "I'd like to get out of this town. Head for warm country." She peered at Andy. "So are you going to look for Regina now?"

"Why?"

Tolliver shrugged. "I thought that's what you came here for."

"It's where I was headed after Columbus, but —" She felt a stirring of excitement. Regina could be tired of Verne. She could have realized Andy was better for her. She could be sick and alone too. "Being gay hasn't been much fun so far. I was thinking, maybe —" She laughed self-consciously, "— of retiring."

"What, from the gay life, girl?" Mandy just laughed.

"But then I start thinking how married I feel to Regina, and, well, she might need me."

Tolliver's eyes opened wide. "You're something else, Blaine, you know that? Nobody needs nobody and we all need each other. You might think about tearing this town apart for your own sake. Just to tie up the loose ends that are bugging you, see how the rest of us queer folk live. I'd be willing to help."

CHAPTER THIRTEEN

"Well, you'll need horns," Starr had said, and now here she was, balancing an embarrassing set of horns on her head, dressed in an old blue coverall with her red sweater stuffed underneath for warmth and heft.

"Who are some of your heroes?" Starr had asked one rainy day while he was sewing his costume.

She thought for a while. Summers she'd loved to bike over to a little cove on the lake. She'd lie there, the scent of pine in her nostrils, watching the *Mt. Washington* cruise in with its horde of tourists, then cruise out with another load, bound for Laconia and Wolfeboro. She'd have a comic book with her, *Superman* or *Wonder Woman* usually, but if she had no money, she'd stop at the library on the way.

"Babe the Blue Ox!" she decided. "I took those Paul Bunyan stories out of the library over and over, until I was twelve or thirteen and the librarian tried to talk me into *Harriet the Spy,* about a stuck-up little city kid."

"Your hero was Babe, not Paul Bunyan?"

"I liked Johnny Appleseed, too."

"Oh, but Babe is the challenge, girl."

The Number 49 bus cruised along Western Avenue toward the Halloween Ball. Andy looked out from her hairy blue mask, smelling rubber, watching the other passengers, none costumed, watch her. Hidden like this she wasn't afraid of anything, even finding Regina.

Starr was more wound up than ever. He was in complete drag — except for the pointy red beard. He wore glitter in his hair, pounds of makeup on his face, and a Cinderella gown. Every time passengers got on the bus he'd leap giddily up and bless them with his magic wand.

Kyle, who'd decided to be a butchy woman, had dressed in an Amelia Earhart costume, but he'd look like a man even if he had worn an evening gown. Andy and Kyle had considered taking the Studebaker, to avoid attention, but Starr had been adamant.

"This is the queens' night out, gang. I'm allowed to be the Great Chicago Fairy on Halloween. If I'm going to embarrass you, go ahead and take the car. I'm traveling by city coach."

Besides, Andy's horns, fashioned by Starr from cardboard gift wrap rolls, aluminum foil, Elmer's glue and blue spray paint, wouldn't fit in that old Studebaker. Clover had yapped fiercely at the sight of her.

"Here we are!" said Starr, literally skipping down the aisle. "Fairy dust! Fairy dust!" he cried, sprinkling an invisible powder. One man cringed to avoid the stuff, and Andy and Kyle stepped off the bus laughing. As the bus pulled away they saw the driver, a woman, wink. A white-haired man waved from a window. A little kid craned her neck to keep them in sight as long as she could.

On the street they passed little Thai, Indian and Filipino restaurants which were perfumed with spicy romance. Would she ever bring Regina back here to sample them? The aging movie theaters looked like old enchantresses decked out in neon. As the strong Chicago winds pushed them along she realized that she felt new, excited, expectant. Around any corner might be the secret formula to life.

The band was blasting from huge speakers. Tolliver danced onstage as she played. The air smelled like popcorn. People turned to look at them. A few peals of laughter, a smattering of applause, greeted their costumes. Andy lowered her head under the great horns, imagining with a sick feeling that Regina was there laughing, but Starr sashayed right into the crowd.

"It really is his once-a-year big moment," whispered Kyle. "He still loves the glamour, whether he's a minister and a feminist or not."

At the dance she watched Kyle waltz Starr around the floor, remembering her first Halloween.

109

"Where's your costume?" the other kids had asked. She'd felt humiliated. Couldn't they see she was a hobo? It was that night she'd realized that she looked like a boy all the time. "Tomboy!" the kids would taunt later at school. She'd feel panicky and fold her hands, cross her ankles, slap her knees together, but five minutes later she was hunched forward on her seat or walking her own natural walk. She really had been a gay kid, just like Frenchy said.

The music stopped. Corn popped madly on the other side of the room. Starr drifted to her side.

Just then Andy caught sight of a profile. Even inside the safety of her costume she froze.

"What is it?"

She stared, lost the face, found her again.

"Is it Regina?"

"No. It's Verne." Her mouth went dry and her knees felt weak. Nausea washed over her like a tidal wave. She had to hold onto Starr's thin arm. *The Knave of Hearts,/He stole some tarts/And took them clean away.*

Starr put his arm around her. "This is it, child, go talk to the cad."

Waves like heat seemed to separate her from Verne. "That isn't Regina she's dancing with." Did that mean they weren't together? If Regina was on her own somewhere . . . Did she really want to find out? What if Regina was free and still didn't want her?

"What are you waiting for?"

"It hurts too much."

110

"Then go back to Weird Beach or wherever it is and hide forever more. You know perfectly well you're here tonight to find her. Get a grip, girl."

Her chest heaved. She wiped the sweat from her forehead with the back of her furry hand. She couldn't breathe inside the horned mask and wrestled it off. The world looked whole and real again and very clear.

"Regina?" said Verne archly, stepping in front of her dance partner as if to hide what she was saying. "She's long gone. You're her back-country butch from Vermont or wherever she came from, aren't you?"

Andy stared at Verne, horrified. "You mean she didn't stay with you?" After, she wanted to add, wrecking everything?

"I have plans, and a hysterical hellcat like your lady did not fit into them. She didn't know what or who she wanted from one minute to the next. She wailed about leaving you, then begged me to take her with me to art school in New York, then followed me here to my folks', would you believe, before I started school."

Verne's features were as sharp, her nasal voice as cutting, as Andy'd always imagined a knave's would be when Gramma recited the rhyme. "Is she still here?"

"Who the hell knows? I haven't seen her. I'm just in town for my grandfather's funeral. She'd better not show up for that. My folks were totally thrilled when that weeping willow appeared at the door the first time." Her partner pulled on her arm. "I'm here to dance. Do you mind?" she said to Andy.

Regina unwanted? "I don't get it," she said, feeling helpless. There ought to be more questions, more answers. "I don't get it."

Starr stepped forward. "One last question," he said to Verne in his authoritative minister's voice. "Did Regina give you any idea where she planned to go?"

"Oh, south, I imagine," Verne said with a shrug. "She complained about the cold, said she didn't have money for winter clothes. I told her to hitch a ride to Tucson where I did my first two years of college, before I transferred to Ohio State. Told her to look up my old girl Feather on some women's land down there. Maybe she's with Feather."

Andy stared as bullfighter-costumed Verne, in the guise of dancing, rhythmically rubbed against her friend. It made her want to barf. Why didn't Tolliver stop playing that sexy sax? She willed the drummer to beat faster and faster with her sticks until Verne, trying to keep up, melted in a pool of her own sweat.

Kyle came over. She let him lead her away.

They got home at about 2:00 a.m. Starr scurried around the house preparing for the New Year ritual. Andy walked Clover, feeling in shock. Tolliver showed up with a friend from her collective, a clown all in scarlet and red. A very young man who attended Starr's church was still in his Cookie Monster costume.

Andy wasn't sure she wanted any part of a ritual. This stuff was just so sixties and all right for Starr and Kyle, but that was practically before she was born. Yet when they opened the circle to her, all of them looking so appealing, she wanted to be part of their family.

Incense wafted across the room. All the lights were out except for twelve red candles in two concentric circles. The costumes — Cookie Monster's blue, Starr's shimmering satin, Kyle's shiny buckles, Tolliver's sharp black and white, and the clown's bright colors blazing in the candlelight — created a warm glow which seemed to draw Andy in, soothe her uncertainties. Life as she'd known it hadn't prepared her for all that would happen to her, maybe these people had something she could use. She joined hands with Tolliver and Kyle and breathed as deeply as she could.

A lightness came into her from breathing. Tolliver's hand felt powerful and calloused, Kyle's strong and smooth. The clown said, "And we ask the Goddess to remove from our path those who want to harm us." The clown went on for a while, then the circle joined in, naming enemies.

"Senator Helms," said Starr.

"Skinheads," hissed Kyle.

The clown's fists were clenched. "Rapists."

Cookie Monster said nothing. Andy sweated, nervous about talking, but she wanted badly to fit in. "Knaves," she said, her eyes on Clover asleep in the corner. She felt lighter still having said it, and stronger. Would the ritual work? Could it help Regina too?

"May our energies protect us all one hundredfold," finished the clown.

Andy concentrated on running a strong circle of white light around everyone there to protect them, as Starr had taught her. When she opened her eyes, though, the clown, in the wavering candlelight, was plunging a knife through a pomegranate. Its red juice trickled to paper towels laid out on the floor. Andy dropped the hands she held and shielded her eyes.

"What's wrong?" Starr asked quickly.

She stared as the clown offered the pomegranate, impaled on its knife, to Cookie Monster. "That looks awful!" Andy replied, lightheaded, as if she were the pomegranate.

Everyone was silent. The pomegranate and knife stayed in the clown's hand. Andy looked from face to face. Was she acting crazy? Would they all dislike her now? It was only a pomegranate already picked, not their enemies, but the knife in it looked so violent, as if they weren't protecting themselves, but wanting to harm.

"You're right," said the clown, taking the fruit from the blade. "It's always bothered me too, like burning in effigy. Let's open the pomegranate instead, and take out the seeds. Maybe we can dry them, bead them, plant them, make a rattle to shake at rituals." She looked at Andy. "Thank you."

"It won't ruin the ritual?" she asked.

Starr said, "No. We're doing a spell of protection, not revenge."

The circle drew together again.

They sang old songs then, quietly because of the late hour. Andy was surprised to recognize some of them from the year she spent in Campfire Girls. This spiritual stuff was so homemade, like Starr's clothing, bits and pieces, remnants of their lives.

Tolliver played a muffled sax. It was no longer

114

sultry, or even jazzy. She seemed to cry into it, through it. At the same time, the music seemed to blanket the group. There was no melody, only the whispery moaning as clear as words. Clover lay against her crossed legs. She wanted to get a group portrait before they left tonight and take this loving feeling with her wherever she went.

Indiana had felt like home, but now so did Chicago. Should she stay here, with Starr and Kyle? Maybe Tolliver would go with her to Tucson. But would this traveling never end? At least she had the money her ma had sent from savings — with an extra twenty-five to make sure she ate well.

Ride a cockhorse to Banbury Cross,/To see a fine lady upon a white horse;/Rings on her fingers and bells on her toes,/She shall have music wherever she goes.

She sighed in surrender. She knew they were right: she belonged with them, she was gay down to her toes. She wasn't Frenchy, she wasn't Verne, she wasn't Tolliver, but she was a lesbian. A lovesick lesbian. Maybe the ritual *had* worked, had made her brave enough to get off her butt and try love all over again.

CHAPTER FOURTEEN

A few weeks later, when Andy climbed into that old Studebaker with Tolliver and Clover, and saw the last that she could of Starr and Kyle waving from the sidewalk, she felt sick all over again. She ached, her voice grew hoarse, and she was shuddering with a cold that seemed to come straight out of her heart.

Once they'd started, Chicago fell behind like it had all been a dream, full of warm and colorful pictures.

Clover sat between them, tongue hanging out as

if she'd been packed for weeks, waiting for this day. The steering wheel felt like an old pal to Andy, warm and worn. With each mile they traveled south she felt her body relax a little more. They'd agreed to take the warmest route they could to avoid bad weather, but Tolliver had an aversion to Texans so they compromised on crossing at the narrow Panhandle. In Memphis Andy peeled off her red sweater. Clover immediately jumped in the back seat and curled up on it.

"She only loves me for my sweater," joked Andy.

"Hey buddy, if it's love don't knock it," Tolliver said.

The first night they slept in the Studebaker at a rest area, but they took their time in the warmth of the second day and only got as far as a tiny town called Shamrock, Texas.

"I need a shower," Tolliver said.

"Do you think there's a motel in a place like this?"

"Probably. With swinging doors and a place to hang your saddle."

"And a cocked horse? Where's the fine lady with the rings on her fingers and toes?"

"Beats me, buddy. Ask room service."

They found a small motel with no other guests. In the lot, Andy said, "Let me get you with some tumbleweed, Tolliver!"

Tolliver posed with one foot resting on a big batch of the stuff, flexing a bicep as if she'd wrestled the tumbleweed down.

They explored the street the motel was on, peering through the broken windows of abandoned motels, looking for the spirits of the ghost town.

"The highway killed this place," Tolliver concluded.

"Look at that!" cried Andy as they approached an abandoned gas station. "It's like the pictures in that museum in Boston."

Andy took a whole roll of the rambling old station with its peeling white paint and red and blue trim. She imagined herself working there in 1947, tilted back on a wooden chair beside a red metal Coke case filled with pop bottles nestled in ice, listening to a wooden radio playing the big bands. Gramma would be home, baking a cake, listening to the same station.

When they reached the restaurant, the people looked as if they were living in the forties. Hadn't they ever seen a Greenpeace T-shirt like the one Kyle had given her? Or a tall black woman in turquoise hightop sneakers and one diamond stud earring? Weren't there other gay people in Shamrock, Texas? She and Mandy Tolliver were such an attraction that the cook, an emaciated man wearing too much hair tonic, spent his break rolling a cigarette and staring at them.

"Not only are they rude," Tolliver commented, "their hamburgers are cooked gray. What do they do, boil them?"

"At least it's warmer here than in Chicago."

"Even if the meal isn't?"

Laughter was their only protection. She was glad Willa wouldn't have to go through this. She heard a whispered *Is it a boy or a girl?* and the guffaw afterward. She heard the names they called Tolliver.

The waitress shoved their plates at them, slopping fries off the edge. Neither of them got straws for their sodas, neither asked. On their way out a heavy man stood suddenly and knocked Andy off balance. He didn't apologize. He came after them. She could see him, filling the doorway, picking his teeth, as they turned the corner.

"We're easy targets with that old car outside our room," Tolliver said.

"What did we do to make them mad?"

"We exist."

"At least now I know why people have always been so freaked out by me."

"You ought to try being black and gay."

"I have my own troubles."

Tolliver laughed. "So you do."

"I hope they don't hurt the car."

"With all the talk of this mondo storm they're expecting I think they'll have their hands full."

The sky was clouding. The tumbleweed seemed to be gaining momentum. "Maybe we should try to beat the storm out of here."

Tolliver shook her head. "These people are trying to run us out of town on fear. I don't want to give them the satisfaction."

Still, crossing the overpass with the wind up and dark settling in as if to stay longer than usual, they hurried toward Clover. *The north wind doth blow,/And we shall have snow,/And what will poor Robin do then,/Poor thing?*

Tolliver switched on the TV, loud. "What kind of town doesn't have cable? These poor hicks can't even

119

get MTV." She switched to *Cheers*. The window rattled. "I don't like the sound of this wind," she explained. "It's doing a danger rap."

"Canned laughing won't drown it out," predicted Andy.

"Then what will?"

They looked at each other.

"Gettin' the fuck out of here," concluded Tolliver.

They piled everything back into the car, turned the local country station up loud and sped out of Shamrock. The newscasts first confirmed the storm's approach, then reported on the dozens of jackknifed trucks and eventually the calling of the National Guard to deal with the blizzard.

They drove all night, taking turns to keep ahead of the storm. At one point Tolliver leaned over to her pack and rummaged.

"There's a woman in Tucson named Windy Sands. I've wanted to talk with her for years. When I read her poem it was the first time I knew I wasn't the only one like me. I wrote to her and she said to come visit any time. I'll give her a call and ask if she knows this Feather person or how to find the women's land. Here, Windy Sands wrote this to a lover," she said, reading to Andy from a ragged magazine.

"*Common Lives/Lesbian Lives*? You mean we have our own magazine?"

"Where have you been, girl? We have lots of them."

Tolliver read aloud.

Who is more womanly
than the stone butch?

Who knows better
how to deny her own
feelings, how to feel
good only when
she's made another to

Who was better taught,
learned more thoroughly?
Who practiced giving
with more ardor?
To kill my own need
I'd stop breathing
before my body felt

They said I denied
my womanhood, when I *was*
their ultimate woman,
knowing only giving,
giving only good,
only good when giving:
womanly; stone butch.

Windy Sands

Tolliver was watching her. "That's what this trip
is all about for me. Only," she complained with a
laugh, "pilgrimages are supposed to be hot, through
deserts and up mountains."

"Pilgrimages?"

"You may not know what you're after, woman,
but I am seeking the oracle. This is, like, spiritual
for me. You know, finding myself and all."

With every mile, now, the air got hotter. Andy's
whole body sighed with relief at the first sign of
green.

"I've got to have a picture. My first real live western cactus!"

As she walked toward it, stiff from tension, she thought about this squat, prickly green thing. Did anyone appreciate cactuses? They were like gay people, living their lives like apple trees or grass, everywhere, but thorny and unwanted. She felt like the cactus, crusty outside, but ready to blossom with flowery surprises in the heat.

Clover watered the silent semi-desert. Maybe she'd been the good luck that got them through.

New Mexico went by like a dream. Although they stayed at another shoddy motel in Gallup, she was so tired she remembered nothing later but the grocery store where they shopped with Indian families.

"I feel like buying myself a ten-gallon hat," Andy said.

They tried some on, from a display in the grocery. "I'm going to hold out for something snazzy and used. We'll get to a thrift store sometime," Tolliver decided.

"Not me," Andy said, pulling an off-white straw hat with a bright band low over her eyes.

"I keep wanting to stop at these roadside places to buy Regina some jewelry." Andy drove one-handed as she scratched Clover who'd insisted on sitting in the front seat with them ever since they'd peeled out of Shamrock.

Tolliver found some jazz on the radio and they fell silent. The rest of the way to Tucson, Andy alternated between dreaming of her reunion with Regina and a life of her own in the desert. Sometimes she pictured herself in her hat, with a red bandanna around her neck, living way out somewhere with no people around. She was a lot older, maybe thirty-eight, tanned from the sun, muscular from mechanic work, and alone when Regina came up to her.

I've been looking for you for years, Andy Blaine.

The heat made everything look shimmery.

Got something for you, Regina. She'd go into the beautiful white Spanish-style home she'd built herself in the midst of green gardens and walk right to the treasures she'd collected. *Here.*

Regina would look at the exquisite turquoise necklaces and bracelets in wonder. *You saved them all these years?*

Them and me.

I'm so sorry I left.

You just wasn't ready, she'd reply with a forgiving western twang and, spurs jangling, move to take Regina in her arms.

"There it is!" cried Tolliver. She rose off her seat in excitement. "*Windy Sands Cactus Ranch.* This is like finding Oz. I wasn't sure the place was real."

* * * * *

"Of course a dyke would raise cactuses," said Andy as she parked in the large open lot.

"So this is how they do it. I expected to find, like, I don't know, a cactus orchard? This looks like an airfield for mini-planes."

A cluster of corrugated plastic buildings with curved roofs housed rough tables made of wooden skids and cinder blocks. Hoses lay everywhere. One building had a sign: Retail Sales Area. Under the light of the yellow translucent roof women of all ages wandered in the humid aisles, collecting what seemed like every kind of cactus there was.

"Look at these colors!" Andy said, taking off her hat to wipe sweat from her hairline. "I always thought cactuses were green."

"Here's one I need for sure," Tolliver said, pointing. "A Ruby Ball Graft." The pretty three-sided plants had huge salmon-colored heads.

"I'd take one of those Painted Ladies home with me," joked Andy about some rounded succulents with waving yellow flowers. There were Desert Roses and Crown of Thorns, Delicate Pinks, Necklace Vines, and Angel Wings. "It's like a flower show."

"Better than any darned flower show," said a loud growly voice behind them. "It's the Magnificent Cactus Circus, is what I call it. Look at them. They're doing somersaults, twirling batons, throwing their firecrackers up to the sky. *Stick with us, we'll grow on you.* That's my motto!" Her laugh was like another bright color.

The woman was tanned and small, gnarled but full of energy. She wore a battered straw hat and her voice was very loud.

"You must be Windy Sands," said Tolliver just as loudly. "I'm Mandy Tolliver and this is Andy Blaine."

"What are you, a couple of Easterners? You never saw cactus before?"

"Not me," said Andy. "The closest I got was in the five and dime back in New Hampshire."

"I never saw a display like this," admitted Tolliver.

A sales clerk interrupted. Windy held her off

while she told them, "Go on back past the ranch. There's some trailers. Make yourselves to home in that big silver one and I'll be out in a while."

They walked past stacks of fertilizer bags, wheelbarrow loads of loam and vegetation Andy could not name.

"This is wild," Tolliver said. "It looks like a shantytown."

"Trailertown is more like it," Andy replied as they came to a halt in front of an older, but well-kept thirty-five-foot Airstream with a wide platform out front. A thatched roof covered the trailer and an eight-foot space in front, letting minuscule strips of sun under its shade. "Nice porch," she said, stretching before she dropped onto a cushioned lounger.

"Ramadas," Tolliver said, walking around the platform, checking the contents of the outdoor refrigerator and cabinets, the barbecuing set-up. "This one's made of juniper branches. Keeps out the sunlight, but lets heat and smoke filter up through."

A while later an open jeep rushed at them and braked hard. "I see you found it all right!" yelled Windy. She used a cane to get out of the jeep and corralled ahead of her two toy poodles.

"Don't either of you Easterners know enough to get up when two femmes arrive?" she asked, taking the lounge Andy vacated for her. "I'd like to present Miss Kitty and Dorothy Lamour. My," Windy said, "look at that dog's ears. You could use one of them for a leash." The poodles ran back and forth between their guests with great agitation. Clover lay at Andy's feet staring as if she'd never seen such alien creatures. The poodles circled Clover, then dared to sniff her. Clover dropped her head onto her paws and went to sleep.

"Whoa, girls!" Windy shouted, laughing with Andy and Tolliver. Her dogs scrambled for cushions set just under the trailer. "They come all unhinged around handsome young butches!" She removed her battered hat. Underneath was a wealth of hair rolled up tight against her head. "Just speak up when you want something. I'm a little hard of hearing and sometimes you might have a tad of trouble getting a word in edgewise. That's how I got the name Windy. I was born Winona Sands. Back when I came out we had lesbian names too, only we called them nicknames. More likely you'd call yourself Duchess or Rusty, than Feather and the other nature names they take now."

Windy's eyes seemed to size you up in a moment, Andy thought, and then welcome you, whatever she saw. She had Andy talking about herself almost immediately, and Tolliver didn't take her eyes off the woman.

"Regina? I've heard that name a lot around lately," Windy said. "Don't look so lovesick, woman. We'll ask Van, my helper, over supper. You gals like Mexican food?"

"If it's hot enough," laughed Tolliver.

"Oh, we've got the hottest of everything down here, Mandy Tolliver."

Andy watched the two of them flirt back and forth for an hour, until the temperature began to sink with the sun, and the desert took on an early grayness.

Windy's assistant, Van Bourne, arrived then, in jeans and scuffed, pointy western boots, striding across the sandy gravel like a large bird coming in for a landing. Her big horn-rimmed glasses perched over a tiny sharp nose and her eyebrows arched way high. She looked startled, like an owl under a flashlight. Her handshake was quick and purposeful. The poodles danced their greeting, then sniffed again at Clover until Windy shouted them back to their cushions.

"Heck of a crowd today, Windy," Van said in a soft voice raised just high enough to reach Windy. She accepted a glass of iced tea.

"Winter," the old woman explained with her flash of a smile. "The snowbirds are swooping down to do their souvenir shopping, shipping half the plants I grow to some cold country where they won't last the season."

"They're like jewels, though," said Andy. "I'd want to take them with me too if I knew where I was going."

"Which reminds me," Windy said, turning to Van. "Does the name Regina ring a bell with you? Lover-girl here," she explained to the guests, "keeps a look-out for all the new faces."

Van raised one of her eyebrows even higher. "Unlike my friend Mizz Windy here."

"I'd say Regina's one you'd notice, lover-girl."

Andy wished they'd stop fooling around. She hoped Van had seen Regina, but not been a lover-girl to her.

"A couple of nights the women from Mesquite Wash showed up at the bar. They had someone named Regina with them. Pretty, with longish hair. Kind of sad-looking and fidgety, like she didn't feel at home here or something."

"When was that?" asked Andy.

"Three weeks, a month ago."

"Do you know a woman named Feather?"

Van looked at Windy. "Some."

"That's who Regina was supposed to visit."

"Feather and I were lovers for a while, but she has a rule about not staying with anyone too long. Tomorrow's the start of my weekend. I can take you over to Mesquite Wash where she lives. You ought to visit it while you're here, even if Regina is long gone. It's an institution, for Tucson and the whole country. Is Regina your girl?"

That was hard to answer. "She was," Andy began. While she told Van the story, she could hear Tolliver telling Windy hers. Tolliver acted like she'd come courting. Windy, shortly before dinner, went into the trailer to change.

"What about Windy?" asked Tolliver.

Van gave her a measuring look. "She's footloose and fancy free." The serious look lifted and she laughed with affection. "And goes at women like a kid in a candy store. Femme, butch, she's not a bit fussy."

Windy came out of the old Airstream in a long robe with loose wide sleeves. She'd taken her hair down and it flowed iron-gray and white across the plum-colored cloth. She looked pretty and not a bit less butch.

After dinner Andy, exhausted, crawled onto her cot. It smelled like Mrs. Kohl's comforter, like Willa, and she almost missed her, but knew she'd done right, saving her from a cactus experience. She fell asleep fighting blizzards, feeling the desert heat, driving, driving, driving.

In the morning she sat up at first light, still tired, but with great excitement peered through the small trailer window. The view was wide open. Today was the day she'd catch up with Regina, she could feel it inside. She patted the cot and helped Clover lumber up beside her. "Lavender clouds!" she whispered. There were traces of gold at the bottom of each of them. The land was a dusky mix of yellow and green-grays. Little bushes, juniper trees and cactuses dotted her horizon. She couldn't wait to see it all with her lover.

She hugged Clover. "Meanwhile, let's show Tolliver!"

But when she turned to the couch, it was empty, the bedding undisturbed.

Andy followed Clover and the poodles outside. Little birds spun giddily from juniper to mesquite to juniper. The January air was startlingly chilly and she leaned back inside to grab her new hat, the old Argus camera and her red sweater. Too bad Willa couldn't see the desert too.

Where was Tolliver? The little birds chittered. Andy wished she could swoop and dive as they did, to warm herself. Instead, she strode away from the trailer, Clover and the poodles in tow.

They walked perhaps half a mile. The dogs sniffed and chased one another as well as everything else that moved. She'd thought Windy was the stone butch in the poem, that Tolliver would just be buddies with her too. Except Van had said Windy was doing it with everyone. Why hadn't there been a course in high school on how to be gay?

Clover was barking at a big gray rock; the poodles barked too, but hung back. Something long, with a dark pattern, slid quickly around the rock.

"Uh-oh," said Andy. "Clover, you horse's ass, get your tail over here."

Clover chased the snake too long for comfort, then presented herself panting, tail wagging like a flag in a hurricane.

"I just don't understand life," she told Clover. "What keeps you safe? Is there a goddess for dogs? How about for lesbians?"

After Andy finished working on an old pickup, she and Van headed over to the west side of Tucson. They had to drive through a national park, dramatic with mesas and saguaros, to get there. The heat of the day was up, but it was comfortable now that she was used to it, almost like spring back home.

It wasn't only the heat, though. Andy was scared of what would come next and felt those Chicago blues all over again. Was Regina chasing excitement out across the desert? Whether she found Regina or not, Andy wanted to settle down like Windy Sands and have something of her own. She closed her eyes and imagined a stream of green light pouring onto her.

Mesquite Wash spread out before them, a house trailer here, a wooden building there, and behind the trees, half a dozen more little homes. There was a ramada outside the main trailer, and lean-tos, an outdoor bathtub. It was like a little world, only instead of elves it was inhabited by women — women with crew cuts and three earrings per ear, women with long hair and ballooning pants with no shirts on, women in overalls, women in shorts, women in nothing at all.

While Van visited a friend, Feather, a tall, gracefully thin woman in a long skirt, light vest and crocheted rainbow cap, took Andy on a tour. Each dwelling was different, some built half underground, some only half-completed. Every one of them seemed crowded with its owner's treasures: big god's eyes, a spinning wheel, clay statuettes, Indian weavings.

Feather's home was more established than the rest. There was only one room, with a separate sleeping loft and a piano in the living area. Andy's first thought was to bring Tolliver to meet her, but she thought better of it. Tolliver had left Chicago to get away from a piano player.

"Sure I know Regina," Feather said, tucking her skirt under her as she settled on a cushioned milk crate. The room smelled of cinnamon. A yellow cat purred loudly beside her and she massaged its neck. "Regina from a little town in New Hampshire."

"Weirs Beach," supplied Andy. "I'm from there too."

"Andy! Of course! She talked a lot about you. Her great red-headed love. So you're tracking her down? Might not be a bad idea. I don't know when Regina will be ready, but my bet is that she will be someday. When she deals with her demon."

Demon? Andy looked at her. "Is she still here?"

"No. She left about a month ago."

Andy let out a whoosh of air. Did she feel relieved or disappointed? Maybe both. "Do you know where she went?"

"Yes. No. One day she'd tell me San Francisco, the next she was headed home."

"Do you really think she went back to New Hampshire?"

"Maybe, but she was hungry to get to the West Coast. You might check with Jenny Alder. That's who Regina was seeing while she was here."

"Seeing?" Andy's gut writhed.

Feather looked at her with sympathy. "Want me to talk to her?"

"No. I'll go. I talked to Verne, the one in Ohio. I guess I ought to see who she likes."

"I wouldn't change if I were you," Feather said, moving to Andy and taking her hand. She had long cool fingers. The look of sympathy in Feather's eyes made Andy wonder whey she couldn't fall in love with someone like her. "She likes you just the way you are and was very sad about not being with you. She's got this demon — I can't tell you more, but she's got some stuff to go through. She has to do what she's doing."

"So do I," answered Andy. She heard nothing else that Feather said. Could Regina have gone back home? *Why?* Regina had hated that town because she couldn't be gay there. Had she stopped being gay?

Andy went outside to pee. Anywhere, Feather had said, but she couldn't. Some naked woman might spring up in front of you while you were squatting there.

She stuffed the toilet paper back in a pocket and

squinted out over the desert. Whoever would have imagined there'd be so many lesbians on the desert. If she stayed here would she become a Windy? Learn to walk around with no clothes on or start wearing feathers and beads? What was so special about Jenny Alder, damn her? She spat.

CHAPTER FIFTEEN

Jenny Alder was at the Womankraft storefront nearby, where an art show was open to the public.

"She's a potter," Van explained. "The work isn't all hers, but hers is very good. I've bought her pots for my own cactuses."

Andy laughed, partly out of nervousness. "Don't you get enough of those at work?"

"I get attached," Van joked.

At the back of the gallery sat a woman Andy's size, with reddish-blonde hair and a squarish freckled face.

"You two could be sisters!" Van exclaimed. "I don't know why I didn't think of the resemblance before. It must be the crew cut that hid it." She looked at Andy, then back at Jenny. "And the ear cuffs. And all those native necklaces. And the beaded vest."

"Don't forget the moccasins," Andy added.

"Jenny is a southwestern Andy," said Van.

"I wonder if Regina noticed."

No one else was in the gallery. Jenny rose and hugged Van.

"This is Andy Blaine."

"Blessed be. Andy Blaine. Your reputation precedes you. I'm glad to meet you." Jenny extended her hand for shaking while she examined Andy. She smelled strongly of some kind of perfume.

Andy hesitated, but shook it rather than be rude. "Do you know where Regina went?" she blurted. She felt sick to her stomach from touching the hand that had touched Regina like that, knowing Regina had held her in the dark, feeling this woman who looked so much like Andy, but thousands of miles away from her.

"Where does anyone go from here? San Fran, sister."

"But where's she staying?"

"I'll tell you, Reggie left in a kind of rush. Didn't really stop to talk, except she'd found something out about herself with Feather and had to leave. I mean, the woman was here one day and gone the next. I mean, a viciously beautiful woman, too. I really went for her. Too hot and cold, though. Dragging me into bed one day, acting like I was a walking germ the next. She *has* to be possessed. You know, spooked out of her head by something. You trying to catch up?"

She wanted to smash Jenny's pots on her damned head one by one and watch her cry. Strutting around like the king of the roost because she'd had Regina. Reggie. What a stupid name for that queen of all women. "I'm thinking about it," she answered, scowling.

"Hey, I'm not trying to step on your toes. I mean, when the woman came on to me I didn't even know Andy Blaine existed. There was some secret she had, something apart from you. She wanted hot sex *and* a shoulder to cry on. Excuse *me,* but I think they're mutually exclusive."

"So you don't have any idea who she might stay with? Maybe on the way west?" asked Van.

"She was talking about a lesbian boardinghouse in the Mission District. Dolores and Twenty-something, is the one I know. Maybe someone out at Mesquite Wash has the word. Just don't bring her back here. I don't appreciate a woman who has no respect for someone's work. She smashed one of my pots on her way out. Into smithereens. Even I couldn't repair it, and I'm good."

Andy tried to swallow her glee at the picture of Regina breaking Jenny Alder's pots.

"Just one?" she asked.

"I got her out before she could put her hands on any more. I mean, all I did was tell her to go back to her small-town love. It annoys me when a woman won't give me all of herself. But this one's in trouble. She's going to have a crack-up if you ask me."

"Thanks," she said, unable to bear being in the same place as this woman.

"Take a look around before you go. Get her a gift for when you find her."

"One of your pots?" she asked, managing to keep a straight face as she wheeled around and flung the front door open.

"Hey!" called Van, jogging to catch up with her outside. "You okay?"

They stopped by a palm tree. Andy played with the stringy pieces of bark.

"I'm okay, but I don't know what's wrong with Regina, taking up with someone like that. I don't know why I thought lesbians had to be good people. Someone just learning to be gay could get a bad impression."

"You have to take Jenny with a grain of salt. She's been in this community forever. She's not about to go away, so you get used to her. And her Paco Rabanne. Besides, you know what Regina saw in her."

"What?"

"You."

Andy was silent, playing with the bark. She slumped forward, forehead against the trunk. "What'll I do, Van? If she wanted me so much she could have had me, she didn't have to come to Tucson looking for a phony. And what do you suppose this secret of hers is? I'm ready to quit."

"Not look for her?"

"Quit love. What good is it knowing I'm gay? The whole world hates me and I can't stand half the dykes I meet. I told about that creep Verne.

Jenny's not much better. How come Tolliver's with Windy? I mean, where are the rules? What about waiting till you're married and all that? What about sticking it out? I don't know if lesbians know how to love; all it looks like they do is sleep around."

Van kicked at the dirt around the tree. "I've got to admit I know what you mean. I don't see where we've got much choice, though. I never learned any rules. What do we do if we're not lesbians? Go with men?"

"Yuk."

"Do you want to be alone?"

"I didn't mind it."

"Well, then. You going back to New Hampshire?"

There was a picture in her mind, maybe a memory, of Gramma opening her arms as if to show her the whole wide world. Opening her arms and blessing her at the same time. *Ride a cockhorse to Banbury Cross.* She took a step back and looked up at the fronds.

It felt like she was exhaling the last year and a half when she sighed. "I guess that's one kind of love," she said. "Family." She was thinking, though, of her dad and how he gave Everett her job. Growing up gay she'd never had a real place in New Hampshire. If she was going to be gay then she ought to stick with the gays in her life. Besides, everybody around here thought Regina was in some kind of trouble. If Regina did have a crack-up, wouldn't she need someone who loved her?

"Do they have palm trees in San Francisco?" she asked Van.

"For sure. You going?"

"I don't know. Maybe I'll get some kind of sign."

A few nights later, they had beans and rice for dinner. The meal was so hot and oniony Andy's eyes teared and her mouth felt seared. She gave Clover her plate to clean and the dog wouldn't touch it.

"I could stay here forever," Tolliver said, patting her stomach. Her wide smile was slack with contentment. She realized that Tolliver's pilgrimage had worked. Tolliver was finding herself.

Behind them the desert hid in darkness. They sat outside wearing their heavy jackets from Chicago. Tolliver wore the black gambler's hat she'd found at the Salvation Army.

"You'll stay as long as I can stand your youth and energy," Windy said with a laugh. "And that shady-looking hat. I expect you to pull a sissy derringer out of your sneaker any minute after you fan your cards." She turned to Andy. "Hand me my mail from the stump, will you? I haven't had a minute to look at it today."

She held each piece of mail up to the light, squinting. "Mail call! Here's one for you, Andy Blaine."

"Who, me?"

Tolliver laughed. "Must be one of those women after your bod."

"No. Maybe my ma. Wait, it's a New York City address." Had Frenchy found Regina? She read the signature first. "Willa."

"Good," Tolliver said. "I always liked the sound of her. I think you'd make a good match. Is she proposing to you?"

Andy read aloud:

"You must be totally amazed that I found

you. If you're still there. I'm in New York, yes, with Frenchy! She's putting me up till I can find some roommates to move in with.

"You didn't think I could do it, I know, so I'm writing to tell you I did. I don't have a girlfriend yet but I'm working on it. There just isn't anyone in the whole of this town I like as much as you. Please send me your address if you move again, Andy, so I can keep in touch. You never know you might want to change your mind and it wasn't easy to find you. I had to go to the 42nd Street Library for your phone book. Your mom was real nice when I called and invited me to visit.

"I have a job in a hotel fifty stories high. People tip here! Frenchy may get me on at her store, though, and then I won't have to commute uptown.

"I don't know what else to say. I missed you real bad after you left. I'd love to hear from you.

"All my love, Willa."

Windy clapped. "That one's got spunk. She's something else, Andy. You wouldn't bring her out so she moved to the Big Apple to do it herself."

"She doesn't know when she's better off. I thought I was doing her a favor!"

"Come off it, Blaine," said Tolliver. "They don't make 'em queerer than you and you wouldn't have it any other way."

There was silence then. The wind slunk low through the scrub. The embers of their mesquite campfire glowed brighter for a moment as if glad to be touched.

"If you go after Regina I hope she's what you want when you get to her," said Windy. Her gray hair was down, but she wore dusty jeans and a red western shirt with pearly snaps. "After all your trouble. I've had some women come out here that seemed to have some demon inside them, driving them to do just the opposite of what they're wanting to do. You ask them why they're moving away, or changing jobs, or leaving their lovers, and they can't tell you."

Tolliver poked at the fire with a long stick. "Out of their gourds."

"That's what it was like," Andy said. "Regina could be content as a kitten and then all of a sudden she'd be crazy to get out and dance with anyone but me, dance dirty, dance wild."

"Then why do you want her?" Tolliver asked. "What are you, Blaine, a doormat?"

Tolliver's anger frightened her. "Sooner or later she'll see that the doormat's still there and the dancers are all gone," Andy stuttered.

"Shee-it."

Windy rose, stiffly, and headed toward the trailer. "One of you drown that fire when you come in." On the steps she looked back at them. "Why don't we take a day off, leave the ranch to Van, and I'll drive you two tenderfoots to see Saguaro National Monument tomorrow. Take Andy's mind off her troubles. I'd love to see just one smile on your face before you move on."

Andy kept Clover awake most of the night tossing on the cot. How would Willa ever make it in

New York City? It was all her own fault for starting things. She could invite her to come to Tucson, or she could return to the city. But she hated it, and Clover wouldn't be safe there. That old Studebaker would probably be stolen and who could afford to live in New York? No, she'd have to bring Willa out here.

She started sweating and her chest ached as she tried to picture Willa on the cactus ranch, Willa meeting Van, Tolliver, Windy. Willa drowning in her arms.

I don't want her, I don't want her, I don't want her!

Once she admitted it to herself she had to wrestle for two more hours with her guilt about fooling around with Willa. She'd needed someone. Willa had wanted to come out. The Kohls had been so nice. And she'd let them down too. The least she could do would be to let Willa come.

In the morning Dorothy Lamour and Miss Kitty, used to rising early now, herded Andy and Clover outside. As she sniffed the dawn air with them she felt an excitement, just under her heart, about the freedom she had. She wouldn't give it all up because Willa dragged on her heart. She walked out further, trying to get the dawn on film.

Then she heard it, a sound like birds, like great slow birds rising by the flock and calling, calling to the sky. They were moving on, too, their wide wings spread, floating, coasting on the air. They were greeting the desert day, singing to the sun, resting on the currents, soaring toward the mountains.

Or was it birds? She didn't see any.

The sun hit a promontory then, and she saw a

figure, tall, dark, with a halo of curly hair, swaying in the new morning light. Mandy Tolliver was out there, playing the soprano saxophone she'd bought used in town. The sax caught glints of light — how had she learned to urge such sounds from it so soon? The horn dipped from her mouth toward the ground as she swayed. Now and then she raised it toward the sky as if in an abundance of emotion. The sound was eerie, lovely, haunting, sweet and sad at the same time.

Andy didn't recognize the melody, but it was as if she knew it, had been hearing it forever. She felt honored to be Tolliver's friend. How could a dyke like herself make such anguishingly exalted sounds?

Andy opened her arms and breathed in all of the pure desert air she could. This was the end of something. Her dilemma about where to go, the pain of Regina, her guilt about Willa, were both tiny compared to the love she felt for life, for the dog resting at her feet, for Tolliver who'd just found herself, and for this golden lavender dawn.

If only, like Tolliver, she was looking for herself. She wouldn't have to trek to any big cities in her search. Then she wondered, so briefly that the thought vanished with the saxophone notes into the air, if it really was Regina, or Willa, that she was looking for.

CHAPTER SIXTEEN

In the Saguaro National Monument Andy left her
friends behind. She walked into a landscape filled
with gray and tan vegetation, red, orange and blue
rocks. After a few steps the silence was so intense
she could hear nothing but the pad of her footsteps
and Clover's name tag against her collar. Where had
all the people native to the desert gone? To city
slums? And why? What had the settlers wanted from
the land, a tourist park? The peace of a land that
went on forever, changing without complaint, losing
without grief?

She looked back. Windy limped next to Tolliver, the two of them looking tiny in the landscape. She and Clover ran to them and stayed close at the monument and through the Desert Museum.

It was late afternoon when they returned to the cactus ranch. The parking lot was nearly empty. Windy pulled her old Jeep into the spot where the Studebaker usually was.

"Where's that old Studebaker?" she asked. "Did you move it, Andy?"

Andy snapped out of a daydream of finding Regina at the other end of the Golden Gate Bridge, arms wide, waiting for her.

Just then, in a cloud of desert dust, the Studebaker appeared from in back of one of the buildings, squealing to avoid hitting an elderly couple.

"Oh no!" yelled Andy, leaping from the Jeep and sprinting toward the New Hampshire plates. "Hey! That's my car!"

She could see the two young men in it stop laughing. They looked at her running toward them, then at each other. The driver floored the gas and sped from the lot.

"No!" yelled Andy from a suddenly bottomless space inside herself. "NOOO!"

"Get the fuck *in* here, Blaine!" shouted Tolliver, half-dragging her into the Jeep.

Clover barked steadily, turning around and around on the seat.

"Didn't you lock it?" Windy yelled.

Andy tried to remember. "Yes, but I left a window cracked because of the heat."

The Studebaker, tuned and full of the new parts

145

she'd installed in Ohio, was well ahead of them. "Oh my God, my car, my car. What'll I do without my car!" Fear tasted like something bitter in her throat. *What will poor robin do then?*

"Keep your pants on, Andy. This old heap doesn't get much speed, but we'll dog them. Those boys can't follow Tanque Verde Road anywhere but town unless — Uh-oh." Windy's hat ties had loosened and the hat was blowing straight back from her head. "They're turning north."

"The Studebaker's not that fast either!" Maybe the slowness that had cost her the race for Regina would win her this one. She hoped the thieves wouldn't blow the motor finding out.

"We better bring out the fire before they get too far up past Sabino Canyon. The Jeep's no good on climbs, and Mount Lemmon's at the other end of this road. Hand Tolliver that shotgun down behind the seat there!"

"Gun?"

"Get it, girl!"

Andy did. "But my car!"

"You want a car with a flat or no car at all?"

She gave it to Tolliver, holding the struggling Clover with her other arm. If Willa came, they wouldn't have a way to get to jobs.

"You ever shoot one of these?" Windy asked.

"Hell, no," answered Tolliver, taking the gun gingerly.

Windy cursed. "You're about to learn then." She issued brief, precise instructions. "Now aim at a tire. I'll see if I can give this thing one last push."

The Jeep was traveling so fast it trembled. Andy's hands curled in fists around Clover's fur. "My car, my car," she chanted to herself, tears rolling down her face. She tried to think of the desert, the lake, to breathe the way Kyle and Starr had taught her. But, oh, her car that had sheltered her, where she'd spent her honeymoon, that had brought her so far! *How will I ever find Regina now?*

"Pow!" went the gun. But they were losing the Studebaker in the foothills. If only she hadn't tried to make the Studebaker as fast as Roy's car. She hated him, hated herself for being dazzled by speed. *The Knave of Hearts/He stole the tarts,/And took them clean away.*

"Pow!" They could hear a smattering of hits.

"Atta girl!" cried Windy. "Damn good thing the *touristas* went home for the day."

It took Tolliver forever to reload.

By the third report they were too far away. They stayed behind the Studebaker, watching for a glimpse of it.

"Damn!" Windy slammed to a halt. "The only thing for us is to turn back and set down at the bottom to wait for them. It's thirty-five miles just to the peak. We'll call the cops and just wait."

"How much gas did you have, Blaine?"

"Guess."

Tolliver smote her forehead and groaned. "A full tank."

It took a long time to find a phone, almost as long for the police to arrive.

"Are you kidding?" scoffed the officer. "They could be up in those mountains for days. There are people who live up there that the Forest Service can't catch."

She watched him examine the three of them:

Windy in her straw hat at the wheel of her Jeep, Tolliver, a rare black person in the white desert town and Andy, in her filling station shirt and shaggy hair, hands in pockets. "You're better off sitting at home, waiting for our APB to snag them on the highway. They'll eventually try to get out of state to sell it. Those classics bring a pretty penny."

Andy spit out the window as he drove away.

That night and the next day she paced Windy's trailer, trying not to cry all the time.

"How can it hurt as much to lose a car as a woman?" she asked.

Windy wouldn't lend her the Jeep. "I'll lend it to you for anything else, Andy, but if you go up in those hills I'll lose you and the Jeep too. I know this country and you don't."

"But I could find it, I know I could. I'd *feel* where it was."

"You'd feel scared to death with this jalopy broken down from the climbing. Besides, you can't feel what's not there. The car's either in Mexico or headed for parts unknown or both. Those guys looked like joy riders to me, though. I wouldn't be surprised if they had no idea how to get rid of her. I think this chase is going to be as wild as your other one."

"And buddy," said Tolliver, "you need to remember it's only a car, even if it is an important car."

"It's not just a car! Everything started with that old Studebaker — my jobs, traveling. Love." Andy knew she should shut up. "You can talk. You have everything you want now. What if there wasn't a

Windy? What if somebody stole your sax and you had no way to get another one?"

There was silence except for her wailing.

Then Tolliver said, "I think you're the nicest, most honest person I've ever met, Andy. But damn, you can be a big baby, chickening out on life when it gets rough. It's always going to be rough. Even if you have Regina *and* Willa *and* a car and everything else you think you need." She went outside with her sax.

Andy blew her nose and watched Windy play solitaire on the fold-down kitchen table.

"I'll tell you, Andy," Windy said without taking her eyes from her cards, "it's all right to stumble around in the dark, but don't complain when you trip on something. Life's got rules like solitaire. I had to learn them, Tolliver's got to learn them — you've got to learn them sooner or later."

"Like what?"

"Like saying no. My girl Jo wanted me to wait till her Dad died and then I could have moved back in with her. Don't you think I wanted to just hole up for the duration to get her back?"

Andy nodded.

"You're right. That's just what I wanted. But there's more to life than a woman who hasn't got what it takes to stick by my side. I would've helped take care of the old man. But she was scared he'd find out she was lez. As if it mattered to him by then what anybody looked like or what their sex lives were." Windy slammed down the jack of clubs. "That kind of life, sneaking around, wasn't for me. People are every bit as much animal as your dog there. They smell your fear and that's when they come tear into you. I wanted a full life with none of that silly hiding."

"So she didn't leave you. You gave her up."

"And got on with my life."

"You think I ought to give up my car and get on with mine."

"Hell no, woman. I think you ought to go after your car. It's those women, Regina and Willa, plaguing your mind that's making you feel so sorry for yourself you haven't the strength to do what you ought to be doing."

"What should I be doing?"

"That's something you need to figure out, not me. But one thing I can do is call my old pal Jerry at Motor Vehicle and ask him to keep his ear to the ground for me."

Two days later Jerry called back. "It's in California," Windy told her. "Around Salton City headed north, driven by one Caucasian male. He managed to elude the local police, but the I.D. was positive."

"That settles it," Andy said.

She'd been walking a lot, taking pictures of the desert plants and animals. At least she'd have a record of where she'd been. She felt like things were getting away from her.

A phrase popped into Andy's head which wouldn't go away: *Give it up or go for it.*

"Regina's in California," she told Windy, "the Studebaker's in California — why am I still here?"

"What about Willa?"

"I can't look for my car in New York."

Tolliver asked, "How'll you get there? Bus?"

"Clover can't go by bus. We'll hitch."

"Girl —" warned Windy.

"I have to do what I have to do," she said with a stubborn pride.

Windy and Tolliver looked at each other.

"Andy, honey, I'm glad you know your mind," said Windy. "We'll give you a haircut before you go. If you don't open your mouth they'll think you're a guy out there on the road."

"As long as I don't get sick I'll be okay. If I ever feel like I did in Chicago, when I'm hitchhiking to nowhere and maybe to nobody —"

"Bad scene," said Tolliver. "You don't ever have to get sick again. Women love you. You have friends. You've traveled more than halfway across the country. You can fix a car. You've got your dog. Plus you're gay and proud like we are. We're here if you need to turn back."

"Yeah," Andy said. "It's different now." She felt harder inside and a little bitter. It looked like there was only one way to learn the rules to live — by living. And only one way to learn how to live gay.

That night, listening to Tolliver pour her liquid music into the dark desert one last time, she wrote to Willa, making it official that she didn't want to be with her. Clover whimpered in her sleep now and then. She'd really liked Willa. Dorothy Lamour and Miss Kitty slept curled against each other at the foot of the couch.

When she opened her eyes the light was out, but there was a flashlight pointed to the floor. "Scared, Andy?"

Andy started, then recognized Windy's voice and bent shape in the dark. "I guess I was asleep."

"That's what I like to see. A strong woman who can sleep instead of worry. You can take care of yourself out there."

"Do you really think so?"

Tears came to Andy's eyes as Windy whispered, "I forget kids have to be told everything. You're okay. You're kind and considerate and lots of fun. I *like* you, Andy Blaine. You're going to make it wherever you land. Don't let anyone bully you into thinking that being a lesbian is bad, especially not yourself."

She could tell Windy was trying to soften her earlier hard words.

Windy chuckled. "Growing up is the hardest thing I ever did. And I'm still doing it."

They looked across the dark at each other.

"Thanks, Windy."

"I'm putting this reference I wrote and your wages by your pack. Here."

She took the flashlight. *"To whom it may concern: Andy Blaine worked for me on my ranch, fixing cars and trucks. She is a good mechanic and a reliable worker."*

"But I just tuned up the Jeep, Van's car and that old van."

"And the pickup. I know a good worker when I see one. You know what you're doing under the hood. The trick is to learn how to do it with your own engine," Windy advised, pointing to her head. "Remember what Nancy Reagan was always spouting about drugs?"

"Just say no?"

"Yes. A trite and stupid woman saying something trite and stupid about the cancer of drugs. But remember the word no when something comes along in life that feels lousy."

Andy fell asleep again, warm with confidence, but awoke at dawn trembling. While she walked the dogs she wished, instead of a job reference, that Windy had written on a piece of paper, *You're okay*.

Her friends drove her out to Route 10. Windy handed her an old blue canvas satchel.

"Here's a thermos of Red Zinger. You can get that refilled anywhere. I put together some sandwiches and a couple days' worth of dog food. You have your car key?"

Andy nodded, too apprehensive about the road, and too sad about leaving, to speak. Tolliver hugged her for a long time. "Be cool."

Windy shook her hand.

Clover panted, watching the cars that came toward them heading north. Andy didn't have the heart to lift her thumb, not yet. She felt utterly abandoned here on the edge of the desert as she watched her pitiless friends drive off.

CHAPTER SEVENTEEN

When the mammoth semi stopped, Andy ran with her canvas bag, suitcase and the green backpack she'd picked up in a Tucson thrift store. Clover strained at her leash and barked at the door that slowly swung open from inside.

"Jody," said the driver, holding out a hand after they were seated.

"Holy Toledo," she said, taking the small rough hand.

"Never see a fee-male drive before?" muttered

Jody, scowling as hard as Andy had on her worst days.

She blushed. "Nothing this big."

"I've been on the road all my grown life. And that's considerable."

Andy looked away from the striking violet eyes set in a web of wrinkles. Jody wore a GMC cap, iron-gray curls pressed out around it. Flicking on her flasher, she worked the gears and pulled out into traffic.

"I suppose you're going to San Fran," Jody yelled over the engine noise.

"How'd you know?"

"I never pick up hitchhikers," Jody said, "unless I know they're members of my club."

"You mean gay?"

The driver gave her a dour look as if Andy'd broken a rule by saying the word. "I'll take you there," said Jody, and fell silent.

Andy sighed with discouragement. Even gay people acted like they hated being gay.

"Picacho Peak," Jody indicated at one point. Later she said, "Casa Grande Ruins." The sun rose to its fullest just past Phoenix, but the cab was chilly with air conditioning. Jody chewed Black Jack gum. Every breath Andy took tasted like licorice. Cactuses and gas stations spiked the land and lulled Andy.

"California."

"What?" asked Andy, startled out of a light nap.

They were pulling off the road.

"This is the first truck stop in California. Maybe you want to let your dog out."

It was mid-afternoon. Sun had obviously been

baking the concrete all day. Andy climbed down to the bleak sight of trucks everywhere, all with engines running. Her eyes seemed to open slowly, letting in more light, more sights.

"*Orange trees!*" she cried into the cement wasteland. "*Orange trees!*" she yelled again, running with Clover toward the nearest ones. She slapped a hand on an orange tree as if playing tag, then raced to the next. "They're real, Clover. Look at these things!" She leaned her head back as far as it could go to study the colorful globes.

Jody had joined her. "I thought you'd feel like Niagara Falls all dammed up," she said with the hint of a smile. "And here you are waking the dead with your trees."

Andy fondled an orange hanging on a low limb, fitting its pitted skin into the palm of her hand. It had the heft of a breast. "It's like meeting Santa Claus. You only see oranges in grocery stores. I guess I never believed they really grow on trees."

"If I had a load I'd take you to the North Pole to meet him too," Jody said. "Why don't you pick one and eat it if it pleases you that much?"

"You don't think they'd mind?" she asked, looking around to see if anyone was watching.

"Come off it, kid. Look at them all over the ground."

She reached to take a fallen orange, smelling the sweet night even through diesel fumes.

"Don't be a dope, kid. Nobody's going to shoot you for taking one right from the tree. Here," Jody said, stooping with some difficulty, "I'll get these for the trip."

Jody cradled several oranges in her arms. She'd

thrown a rotten one for Clover who pranced back from fetching it, the open fruit dangling from her mouth. Jody turned toward the truck with her booty. Was that how she, Andy, looked to other people? Scowling, silent, sitting on the life in herself, scared?

She followed Jody and put Clover in the truck, then headed to the bathrooms. Once in a stall she realized she did feel like Niagara Falls. It had been six hours since she'd left Windy's. How far would they drive today? Would Jody be upset if she asked? Was she being a big baby to feel afraid of her? If only she had that old Studebaker back she wouldn't have to be depending on scary strangers.

"Let's chow down," muttered Jody after Andy fed and watered Clover.

They sat on stools at the truckstop counter. "Never trust anything but the eggs and fries unless you know the stop," Jody said. She ate with her face low to the plate, her eyes on the food. Was that tightness around her eyes the same fear that cursed Andy? When Jody did look up it was with short covert glances, even at the salt shaker, which she shook over her fries for a very long time.

Damn, but this woman felt familiar, shoulders hunched around a hurt in her chest. Andy remembered the Holiday Inn snack machines, how cowering she must have looked before them, and the gas station, the body shop, high school where she'd kept her eyes to the ground, not an unnecessary word to anyone. She'd arrived at Starr and Kyle's doorstep sick with fear. What a bimbo she was: she wasn't afraid of Jody, Jody was afraid of her.

Jody surprised Andy by sliding a quarter into the jukebox and puncturing the sound of clattering dishes with Linda Ronstadt's "You're No Good," then Anne Murray's "You Needed me," two oldies that Regina had liked.

"Do you have a friend at home?" she asked Jody.

Over a coffee mug the violet eyes cut her like disapproving swords. "Died."

"I'm sorry," said Andy as quickly as she could, but she wasn't sure whether she meant because of the death or her question.

"Ten years last month."

"I'm real sorry." Had the woman always been silent, or just since she'd lost her lover? Ten years without Regina or even the merry Willa and who'd remember how to talk, much less want to? The woman must live all alone, Andy decided, getting up for her job, eating only to stay alive, lost. But why, then, the jukebox? Did the music date back to her lover?

They both grabbed toothpicks on their way out. A woman crossed the lot toward them. She was brightly made up, pants tight, on little high heels.

"Jody! I *thought* that was your truck!" She threw her arms around Jody and found her lips. "You devil, you. You haven't been out this way in six months."

Jody reset her hat and chewed her toothpick double-time. "They've been sending me on a regular route to New York City."

"You must have been busy parallel parking with the girls back east then. Did they make you forget about Dorita?" She was clinging to Jody's arm.

"Naw. You're still my best gal, Dor."

"Can you stay a while, sugar?"

"Naw. Gotta get this load up to San Fran by

tomorrow. Besides, I have a rider. What's your name there?"

"Andy."

"Andy, meet Dorita."

"You ever want a good time, Andy, you look me up."

Dorita stuck her tongue in Jody's mouth when she kissed her goodbye. "Maybe on your way back, sugar?"

"We'll see."

Dorita waggled her bottom into the restaurant. Andy looked at Jody. There were two or three hookers who worked Weirs Beach summers. Everybody knew who they were, and they all worked out of the same house. Now and then one would appear on the boardwalk pushing her baby in a carriage, or at an arcade with another hooker, playing the electronic games, using the fortune-telling machine. This lady looked and acted just like them.

Did Jody — did lesbians — go to hookers?

"Don't keep staring at me," Jody said over her toothpick an hour later when they'd passed through another eternity of desert. "She's one of the nicest gals you'll ever meet. You don't have to go to any bar and make a lot of chit-chat to go with someone like Dorita. And it's not a money proposition with her. She likes it with women."

Andy didn't know what to say. Dorita probably did nothing worse than Regina, and she was almost as pretty.

"The Chocolate Mountains out there," Jody said, pointing west.

It was well into the night when they skirted Los

Angeles, but they still ran into traffic. Jody found another truck stop. "We'll sleep till about three," she told Andy, climbing into the bed behind the seats and setting the alarm on her big black watch.

Andy walked Clover alongside the highway, stumbling, her legs half asleep. Jody had pointed out the Joshua Tree National Monument and Palm Springs, but had otherwise been silent, intent on her driving. Jody listened to her CB, but never talked into it.

Did she have friends aside from Dorita? Family? How had she become a truck driver? It was something Andy had never considered for herself, and now, after meeting Jody, she knew it wasn't a choice. She didn't want to be lonely ever again. She wanted other people to like her, even if it meant changing things she didn't know how to change. No one liked a big baby, not even her. She was getting along all right without her car or Regina or Willa.

The trucks roared by, the palm trees and fruit trees posed in the moonlight, she was riding in a cross-country truck with a stranger. It was pretty exciting. Regina had given her much more than a year of love.

Where was Regina now? Still crazy with restlessness? Still unable to finish the loves she began? Wouldn't she have been thrilled to ride in a truck through the night. She wished for Regina, but, hey, like Tolliver and Windy said, two women had loved her and she did have friends.

She turned back, afraid she'd wake Jody if she stayed out too long, but not wanting to enter the closed little world of the cab. It felt contagious,

Jody's life, and as anxious as Andy was about the future, she felt even more frightened of her past. Surely she could have more for herself than Jody had? She took pictures, using her flash under the fluorescent truckstop lights, of Jody's truck.

In the truck, Jody snoring behind her, she twisted and turned so much Clover moved to the floor. Every time she fell asleep she had nightmares.

In one, Tolliver and Windy were driving away, leaving her and Clover by the side of a highway without a car. Then it was Ma and Dad driving away, leaving her with Gramma. Then it was her, Clover and Gramma, on the side of the road dodging big trucks. Clover was hit, Gramma was hit. Andy stood alone while a truck barreled toward her. It had a name on it in red script that looked from a distance like "Andy."

"No!" she yelled. This was the one that was going to get her. "No!" she screamed, anticipating the crushing pain of the blow. Then she saw the name. It was "Jody," not "Andy" at all. She woke with such a sense of relief and gratitude, all mixed in with grief at her losses, that she prayed to gods or goddesses or anything to help her know what to do.

Several hours later Andy left the cocoon of the truck at a BART station in Oakland at the height of the commuter rush.

"Don't take any wooden nickels!" Jody shouted. She hadn't let Andy take her picture. The truck wheezed and groaned through the traffic toward the docks. Andy leashed Clover and lifted her three bags. Jody had advised sneaking the dog across the bay on the BART. She felt scared, but it was either that or stay in Oakland. If only she had that old Studebaker.

"Let's go, Clover!"

Under cover of the crowds, who seemed both cheered and challenged by the novelty of smuggling a smiling dog, they made it to the Embarcadero Station.

Wasn't it just yesterday that she'd sat inside the Hungry Bear Restaurant on Lakeside Avenue in Weirs Beach and had her usual breakfast? Now she'd crossed a bit of the Pacific Ocean! She took pictures of the water off the Embarcadero, then walked along Market Street. Tying Clover outside a tinselly little shop, she bought postcards for Tolliver and Windy, Starr and Kyle, her folks and, changing her mind three times, Willa. Through a loudspeaker the shop next door played the sitar music Starr had liked.

In this blue-gray city the air tasted different. It was wet with the fog she'd seen billowing on the bay, but touched by sun that worked hard to burn through. She and Clover walked till noon along Market Street, stopping on a bench at the Civic Center to eat the last of the food Windy had packed. She'd filled Clover's little bowl at a water fountain. A clown in red and green pranced through the crowds greeting pedestrians, waving at drivers and giving lollipops to little kids. Andy photographed the clown's brightly painted face and gaudy ruffled clothing against the white buildings.

San Francisco must be Banbury Cross itself,

Andy thought. Jangling with traffic and jingling with excitement, it looked like it had rings on its fingers and sounded like it had bells on its toes.

She waved goodbye to the clown and headed for the lesbian inn. Her directions told her to turn at Dolores. What a fairyland! Huge palms swept along the corridor of the enormous street. At every corner she paused to look down steep hills. Back home she'd watched every rerun of *The Streets of San Francisco*. The city was even better in real life. The Bay winked at her in the distance; the bright buildings seemed to dance up and down the hills; the sun alternately heated and chilled her, as if there were a giant thermostat hovering somewhere. Orange trees, lemon trees, limes, flourished in backyards. She might not like cities, but there was magic here.

What if Regina was at the inn?

The thought didn't panic or excite her. Regina hadn't been anywhere else, why should she be here? Even if she were, she was probably seeing some geeky woman who wouldn't last.

Andy's calves ached from walking. Her eyes smarted from city air and from looking. She refused to worry about what would happen if there wasn't a room available. She rang the bell at the inn. Every piece of wood seemed to be painted a different color. The windows were so full of plants she wondered if sun could filter through.

"Come in!" called a voice from an open window above her head.

She stood in the entryway, waiting, squinting at

the old-timey furniture, the mismatched rugs, the tall windows, the paintings and drawings on the walls, all of women or animals.

"I'm Andy Blaine," she said. "Jenny Alder sent me."

The innkeeper had short curling blonde hair and lines on her tired face. She smiled in a distracted way and led Andy to the living room. "Jenny Alder?" she asked.

"From Tucson."

Rustling through some papers, the woman combed her hair with her fingers and reassured her cats about Clover all at the same time. "I probably remember her, but that's all right. You need a room?"

"We both do."

"You and your lover?"

Andy panicked for a second. "Lover? Is Regina — Oh, you mean — No. *Clover*," she explained, pointing down.

"Of course. She's no problem. Katy and her Dalmatian Rover — or was it Rover and her Dalmatian Katy? Right, Katy's the dog. I never could get that right. I was always calling the dog Rover. In any case, Rover and Katy moved to Anchorage last week so their room is empty. What can you afford?"

They set a price and the innkeeper showed her a huge room on the third floor with a window looking north and a futon covered with a Navaho bedspread. There was storage under the eaves. She could see the bay from the hall bathroom, if she opened the stained-glass window. They went down the hall and around a corner to the kitchen. A tiny black woman in baggy shorts and a T-shirt smiled as she stirred something full of garlic.

Back downstairs Andy said, "If you hear of any mechanic work, I'm looking for a job."

"I'm sure I have what's-his-name's card around here somewhere — he works out of a garage. Here, by the phone, I've been meaning to call him about my car. Why don't you look at it? I haven't been able to start it for two months and I'm going to Santa Rosa next week. If you can fix it we'll barter around your rent. I don't know, though, it might have been last year he was looking for help and I suppose I could take a bus."

Thoroughly confused, Andy lifted her bags to go upstairs. "What's your name?" she asked.

"Of course," said the innkeeper and rummaged in her desk again. "My card."

"Meg Klein," Andy read aloud. She for sure never met another lesbian like this one. She was more like somebody's ma. "Thanks."

"And here, this is the mechanic's card."

It was now or never. She stuttered out her question. "Does a woman named Regina stay here?"

"Regina?" Meg Klein stared out the window for a long time. Had she been with Regina? Was she going to break down and talk about how broken-hearted she was when Regina left too? "I have to get someone in here to fix that window. See how the frame's shrinking? Who were you asking about? No. I don't remember a Regina. Ask some of the other women, though. I sometimes forget my name, never mind theirs."

Good, she thought. For some reason she didn't feel she had time for Regina right now. Tolliver had gone to Tucson to find herself. Andy had a feeling that San Francisco would be her Tucson. She wasn't ready to see Regina.

"Isn't that funny?" she asked Clover who was patiently waiting for dinner. "When I wasn't much of anyone at all I would have thrown myself at Regina. Today, I'm not going to throw any part of myself anywhere. Not till it's all accounted for and passes inspection. Big baby indeed. Was that why Regina left?"

The rent had taken all but fifty dollars of her money. She fed Clover and filled a bowl with water, unpacked her odds and ends, and went into the kitchen.

"Andy Blaine," she said to the tiny woman who was washing her lunch dishes. The T-shirt said Dyke University. Was there really such a place? Here in San Francisco anything was possible. In the kitchen, another woman, tall and gangly, wore a flannel shirt open over a men's undershirt and drawstring pants.

"Cricket," said the tiny woman.

"Umeko," said the tall one.

"Where you from?" asked Cricket.

"New Hampshire."

"Way back there? You must have been on the road a while."

"Going on two years now."

"I'm going traveling some day. I was born in Oakland and only got this far."

"Don't bother," Umeko said. "I left San Francisco for four years and went to college in Michigan. Weird. I won't leave here again in this body." She

166

was scrubbing a pot that may have had oatmeal in it. "You'd think they'd never seen a Nisei before."

"A what?"

"At least you're honest. Second generation Japanese-American."

"We didn't have anyone Nisei in Weirs Beach."

"How about black people?"

"Once in a while during tourist season. There isn't much reason for anyone to come to Weirs Beach anymore. The amusements are all gone and we don't have all those cute little shops like in Meredith. Just the arcades and the old-fashioned guest houses. And the lake."

"How come you're not in culture shock?" Umeko asked. She sounded like she might be making fun of her. Andy felt a warning stir of anger.

"What do you mean?"

"San Francisco must be radical for you. We ran all the WASPs out of town."

"Listen, I just think people are people, okay? I'm not going to bug you about what you are and I hope you're not trying to get to me either." She was hot with sweat.

Umeko smiled and stuck out a hand. "I guess I asked for that."

"She's got an attitude and a half," Cricket confided.

Umeko sat down with a hand to her head and explained, "I work in corrections and I put up with a lot of assholes, mostly not the ones behind bars. South Africa just let Nelson Mandela out of jail after decades of keeping him locked up for nothing, yet in

167

this country juries acquit child molesters. Kids don't make up stuff like that! I just don't want to come home to total ignorance."

"Sometimes I feel pretty ignorant," Andy confessed, "but not about important stuff."

Umeko offered a chunk of tofu to Clover who chewed it and left it on the floor. They laughed. Andy cleaned it up.

"Do you know where Chattanooga Street is?"

"Not far from here," said Umeko.

"What you looking for there?"

"The card says Nicholas Autoworks."

"Oh, Nicholas! Sure, I know where he is." Cricket gave her directions. "He's a great mechanic, but sooo granola."

"A good dancer though!" Umeko added.

The walk was short. Andy reveled in the giant aloe plants and the bell-shaped red flowers and the huge white trumpets that poked up from staircases and decks. Clover met her first Afghan hound. As they rounded the corner to Chattanooga Street she realized that she'd stood up for herself and it'd gone just fine. Umeko had been testing her. That didn't feel okay, but she wasn't out to change the woman. At least she wasn't scared of her now. She also hadn't remembered to ask either of them if they knew Regina. She'd been too busy trying to be herself.

Nicholas Autoworks didn't have a sign. It seemed to be in the garage of a tall dirty white stucco house. The garage door was painted salmon to match the framework on the house and the steps. She stooped under the door, which was half raised, and looked around. The space opened from single car width to double in the back, with columns between stalls. She was surprised to see a pit under a Monte Carlo just as there would be in a professional garage. Opera music played from an elaborate stereo system on the side wall.

"Can't take on any more repairs for two weeks unless you brought me a helper," came a voice from under the Monte Carlo. There were also a Volkswagen and a Subaru Justy stuffed inside the garage.

"Good," said Andy, smiling. "Then you'll have to hire me." Her encounter with Umeko had made her feel confident.

Nicholas climbed out of the pit, hands covered with oil. He pulled off his Pennzoil cap, and gray curly hair puffed out over his jutting ears. Gray- and black-striped overalls hung from his massive shoulders and stretched across a small pot belly. He had to be six-foot-five. His feet alone were as long as Clover's tail.

Had anyone said he was gay? None of Frenchy's, Starr's or Kyle's friends were massive like this. Except for the longish hair he could be in that restaurant in Shamrock. A smile stretched across his basset-hound face like a gleeful half moon. Clover, after some hesitation, wagged her tail. Andy didn't blame her. Nicholas felt like sunlight on a winter day.

He appraised Andy, head to toe. Over the music he said, "Wild. Are you any good?"

"Pretty good. I have a reference." She held out Windy's recommendation. "My Dad taught me. He ran a garage. Then he took on my brother and there wasn't room for three."

"So you took off."

"No. I stayed and painted cars, trying to get on someplace else, but Weirs Beach is pretty small."

"So then you took off."

"Not till Regina."

"Gotcha. Come on under here and see what you think."

She scooted under the Monte Carlo. "I don't think they ever changed this oil before, for one thing," she told Nicholas.

"He said he added to it, but never got around to changing it."

"There's more stuff clogged down here than —

"He wants to know why it's sluggish."

She looked up from under the car at Nicholas and laughed. "He can't figure out —?"

Nicholas began to laugh too. "No. He's a computer programmer, thinks you ought to be able to put in a clean disk and —" He couldn't finish for laughing. "It's been so long since I had anyone to sound off to about —" He broke up again. "They ought to issue a license for owning a car, never mind driving it!" He grinned and shook his head. "I don't suppose you have any tools."

"Some. Not a whole lot."

"You're in luck then. The fella that worked with me last had to retire early. AIDS. He donated these to the shop. By now, though, he could probably use the money. Maybe you can pay for them as you go."

Her first task was to clean up that Monte Carlo. It ran fine afterwards, and she went back the next morning to discuss wages with Nicholas.

He was in the same striped coveralls and smudged cap. This time Andy noticed that Nicholas had two bright gold dog teeth. Umeko had said that he was gay, but Andy had never seen anyone so masculine in her life. How many other men had she assumed to be straight when they weren't? How about the men in Texas?

After she secured Clover to a railing just outside the garage door, Nicholas told her, "I can give you a percentage. That means if it ever gets slow you'll have to bring in your own work, but I don't pay taxes so you won't have to either." He lowered his voice. "This is an *underground* business, so until this country gets universal health care I can't do a health plan, but you can probably join mine, it's the cheapest around. Covers practically nothing except if you're about to die." He narrowed his eyes at her and pushed out his lips, as if deciding whether to say more. "Do you smoke?"

"No," she said.

"A-mazing. I do a little toke now and then, on my lunch hour."

"Doesn't bother me." Then she realized what he was saying. "Oh. You mean marijuana."

"I know a lot of lesbians don't go for that these days."

She shrugged. "I guess it's okay. I never did it. The smell's a little nasty."

"No problem. I've got an exhaust fan for the fumes in here anyway."

As they talked Andy noticed the yellowed poster of Fidel Castro and one of Chairman Mao on the back wall. Under the posters, like wallpaper, were dozens of Doonesbury cartoons. She wasn't going to have much in common with Nicholas outside of cars.

"You like the decor?" asked Nicholas, the crescent

grin back on his face. "Late sixties revolutionary. I suppose it's time for a change, but I haven't found any new heroes yet."

He said it with an apologetic tone. Is this what had happened to all those student revolutionaries Dad used to laugh at? They work in garages? And now she was going to work with one and not pay taxes? Dad would be proud of her. He was always slapping bumper stickers on his car like the one that poked fun at the New Hampshire license plate motto: *Live Free or Die? They're Taxin' Me to Death!*

San Francisco wasn't all that far from home after all, except it *was* magic. Maybe she'd lost her girl and her car, and didn't have much, but life was turning around. A room and job just like that. And why not? She had some say in her life. All she had to do was say no. Or yes.

There was so much work backed up she didn't have time to think about Regina or to explore the city for a week and a half. Sometimes she nearly sang with the opera she was so glad to be working on cars — and for a queer.

"Maybe we can take Sunday off," Nicholas said, after they'd worked from 8:00 a.m. to 6:00 p.m. ten days in a row.

"I'm enjoying myself."

"It was my lucky day when you walked in here. I don't want to spoil you with a whole day's R&R, but if I wear you out I'll never find another Andy. You're worth your weight in gold. There are a lot of mechanics out there, but most of them think these are mere personality-less machines we work on."

"That just gives me today to get this poor old VW singing again before we take off."

Nicholas laughed. "Ah, a mechanic who can hear song in an engine. What're you going to do with your day off, fix your own car?"

The idea of a day off scared her a little. She'd already put the new battery into Meg's car. She'd written out the postcards over supper one night, but hadn't heard from anyone, and she'd stocked up on groceries around the corner in Noe Valley on her way home one night.

"No," she answered. "I guess I'll start looking for it."

"You're in the market for one?"

"I want to find mine."

"What happened to it?"

"Somebody stole it back in Tucson."

Nicholas whistled low.

"The police say it came to California. It's an old Studebaker Hawk. I thought I'd check with them."

"That won't do any good, but I have some other ideas. Want help?"

"All I can get."

"Let's switch that day off to Monday when the shops are open and we'll see what underground San Francisco turns up."

* * * * *

They didn't get back to the garage until Thursday.

Nicholas was like that, it seemed. When he bit into a job, he didn't let go until it was finished. Wednesday afternoon at ten of four, he got a line on what might be that old Studebaker.

They'd stopped at a grungy-looking gas station in

South San Francisco. Andy sighed in relief when Nicholas turned off the opera they'd been listening to. It was one thing to listen to the stuff in a big garage, but closed inside the small pickup cab it was too much.

Nicholas wore jeans and a red striped jersey. His curls were silver and thick. Usually Nicholas talked with the mechanic, but this time he leaned out his pickup window to the most ancient pump jockey on earth. Old Johnny was stooped, as if he'd leaned over motors far too many years. He didn't talk without spitting tobacco first.

"You're barking up the wrong tree, Nick. These kinds of guys —" Old Johnny indicated the littered station with a hand curled by arthritis, "— don't know Studebakers. Hell, they think cars went from your Model T to your 'Vette with nothing in between. No, you want to be checking out some of these fancy dudes around the car fairs, you want to see your Studebaker again. They're not above a little hanky-panky to fill in the holes in their collections."

As he scratched Clover under her collar he gave them a name and the date of the next show, which was two weeks away, and would be held three hours south.

"It's enough to make a cat laugh, how little these young upstarts know about cars," he went on, glowering at Andy. "Except your friend Nicholas here. Never met a fella smarter at cars, even if he is the ugliest grease monkey I ever saw." As they began to drive away Old Johnny yelled, "Bet you didn't know Studebaker started out building covered wagons! Half of us Californians never would've got here without those Studebaker Brothers!"

She went with Nicholas to the Artemis Cafe.

"I don't know why I didn't think of the car fair crowd," said Nicholas. He chewed an enormous bagel sandwich with as much ardor as he'd bitten into the search for the car. "My old prejudices, I guess. You know, if it's stolen look at the poor people."

She noticed a woman out of the corner of her eye. It wasn't that she looked like Regina, but she had an air about her, a very feminine prettiness that stood out among the punk haircuts and the studded wristbands and the pierced ears.

"Is this where all the women in San Francisco come for dinner?" she asked.

Nicholas laughed. "Not hardly. There are thousands of lesbians here. Tens of thousands."

"It feels so different, not being the only one."

"Freaky. Believe me, I know. We'll go over to Amelia's afterwards where you can see more dykes. Why waste a parking space? The women know me there."

She hadn't dared to hope that the woman with the air about her would show up at Amelia's too, but she did. Like Regina, she had a wonderful strong nose, but hers was narrow with a tiny bump high up. It was set in a pixie-like face with smoke-blue eyes and aviator style glasses. Her hair was short and straight, maple syrup brown and very fine-looking, the kind that would follow a comb anywhere. If Regina was an ad for designer jeans, this woman modeled for Ivory soap. Gramma would like her, she thought.

"Holy Toledo," she said.

"Where?"

"In the white blouse and jeans."

"Nice-looking lady."

"Do you know her?"

"Nope. You're going to have to do that on your own, amiga. But there's someone I do know."

He waved Cricket over.

"Thought I'd drop by early before the action started," Cricket said, still in baggy shorts, and wearing a different T-shirt which read *Does Your Mother Know You're Out?* "But I see I'm too late, they're piling in."

Nicholas leaned toward Cricket. "Do you know the lady in the white shirt?"

"Of course. That's Jasmine Jones, one of the nicest women in San Francisco. Always a smile and a big hello. She's an R.N. Why — you're not her type," joked Cricket, looking at Nicholas' body. "You are too hairy, woman."

"Maybe Andy would fill the bill," Nicholas suggested.

"She's a nice kid, Andy. You a heart-breaker?"

Andy felt her cheeks flush as she thought of Willa. "Not on purpose."

Cricket pushed away from the table. "Let me get a Calistoga and see if she's here with somebody, wants company, the whole bit."

While Cricket was gone Andy fidgeted, trying to avert her eyes from the woman. Why had she opened her mouth about her? There was no room in her life for someone new. Right this very minute she was supposed to be looking for Regina. She looked around the room. This was where she'd be all right.

Of course, Jasmine Jones might not like her. Why should she? A gawky country bumpkin chasing another woman who didn't want her across the

country, turning her back on one who did want her
and losing her car along the way?

Cricket brought Jasmine Jones back to the table
and made introductions, then pulled Nicholas to the
dance floor.

Holy Toledo, thought Andy. She drummed both
feet on the floor and all her fingers on her bottle.

"Are you from San Francisco?" she asked, certain
it was the only question she'd be able to think of all
night.

"No, Winooski, Vermont."

"New England? You're kidding!"

They talked about their lakes.

"I used to take my little brothers out fishing, but
all we ever got were sunfish," Andy said.

"My father had a small sailboat. He took us out
on Champlain in summer, and we ice-skated in
winter."

"We went to smaller places to skate.
Winnepesaukee's just too big to trust."

"Pom-poms on white lace-up skates —"

"Black racers. The other girls laughed, but I beat
all the boys because I was lighter —"

"The tourists in the summer —"

"The quiet —"

"The peace —"

"The boardwalk —"

"Autumn —"

"The maple trees —"

"You don't have an accent!"

"You just have the same one!"

They laughed their way onto the dance floor. Jas
felt like a lake breeze in Andy's arms, crisp but soft.
She was just a little shorter than Andy, and lighter

by not many pounds. Her glossy hair felt like cobwebs against Andy's cheek. She told Jas about being a mechanic and owning that old Studebaker.

Jas laughed. "I took all the money my grandparents ever gave me for my birthdays and Christmas and bought an old Nash to commute to nursing school."

Before they left the floor, several songs later, Andy had told her the story of her cross-country trip — and Regina.

"I'd love to see your car when you find it."

"You'd look good in it."

Jas had a way of tilting her head and letting her eyes catch the light. They were smiling, as open and clear as little lakes. Her manner was kittenish.

"I have to get up for work," said Jas finally.

She couldn't let her go. Jas was so easy to be with. For the first time Andy really felt gay. "Where do you live?"

"Collingwood Street, off Twentieth. Not far from Nicholas' garage."

"Can I walk you home, Jasmine Jones?"

"Only if you'll let me give you a cup of tea."

They sang songs from Willie Nelson's *Blue Skies* album all the way up the hill. Jas had a surprisingly loud singing voice and a nice girlish wiggle to her walk. Collingwood Street was so steep it had stairs instead of a sidewalk.

Her apartment was on the third floor of an old wooden house and consisted of a room about the size of Andy's with a separate kitchen and a bathroom.

"I don't have much furniture yet. When I moved in, my ex had enough for both of us. Do you want to come shopping in the secondhand stores with me this weekend?"

"If Nicholas didn't have too much for me to do I was going to start looking for Regina." Jas was no butch buddy. She couldn't ask her to help.

"That's too bad. I can borrow a VW van this weekend. I have a cousin here who's been really great about helping me get started on my own. His boyfriend just died of AIDS."

"Wow."

"What kind of tea? Peppermint?"

"Anything."

"You're not too hard to please."

She told herself she would not fall in love because a woman happened to cross her path her first night on the town. She reminded herself about *Just say no.*

Watching Jas move around her little kitchen, though, where everything was just so, reminded her of home. It even smelled like Gramma's kitchen, before she had gotten sick and moved in with the Blaines. This is only a cup of tea, not a proposal, she thought, as Jas brought it steaming to her.

All Andy could do was grin across that kitchen table.

CHAPTER EIGHTEEN

Thursday morning, as she and Clover walked to Chattanooga Street, it seemed like even more flowers had popped out. Either that, or the ones already there had grown more brilliant. Andy hoped Regina was in San Francisco to see them because she'd never be able to describe their colors and abundance. The red blossoms on a tree in front of one outrageously pink and maroon and aqua building looked just like the bottle brushes her mother had always had on the sink.

"Have a good time?" asked Nicholas with a wink.

She felt herself blushing. "How long did you stay?"

"That little Cricket took me over to the Rawhide and wore me out after a dozen country dances. She can't dance to rock at all, but give her steps and she turns into a regular Ginger Rogers."

"I wish I'd seen you two." She laughed to picture long-haired, big-bodied Nicholas out there with Cricket hopping beside him. *Jack, be nimble,/Jack, be quick,/Jack, jump over the candlestick.*

"Wild," said Nicholas with a gold-toothed grin.

"You were too busy looking elsewhere." Nicholas put his cap on. "Let's get to work."

It was so good to be working on cars again, even with those opera singers reaching for incredible notes as she reached for hidden nuts and bolts. It wasn't country music, but she was starting to be able to sing along with the good parts. "Toar-ray-a-door!"

She planned to bring her camera to record every detail of this dark commonplace garage which was like paradise. The fan belts looped over nails on the wall, the caged lamps hooked to the cars, the delicious oily hot-motor smell and the feel of vinyl over car seats, the ridged rubber mats, the whir of power tools replacing tires, the clang of a metal tool falling on cement — what more could she ask?

She thought about Jas all day, but couldn't remember what she looked like or exactly what they'd said. It was as if she'd had a pleasant dream the night before, about a Willa already out and exciting, or a Regina who was nice, and laughing, and fun to be with. Was there such a Regina in the world? Could she really love someone else as much? That would make being gay worthwhile.

181

She wanted to walk with Jasmine and Clover past the flowers on the hillsides, and the bottle-brush trees, and the gussied-up houses. At lunch she called Jas at the hospital where she worked. Yes, Jas said, she started at seven a.m. too, so if they both got off at three they'd have some daylight left. She asked Andy to come by after work and they would buy French bread and cheese and fruit to eat along the way.

Jasmine Jones likes me! Andy thought. The words turned into a little song which she hummed inside her head all afternoon while she worked. Even the dirty oil draining into a pan sang the same song. The search for Regina could wait a little longer.

When she went home to change and wash off the grease that afternoon, she found a letter from her ma Meg had left at Andy's door.

Dear Andrea,

It was good to hear from you. You know I'm not much on letter writing, but it's been a while since we got that last card from California and your Dad and me were wondering where you'd got off to now.

The boys stick your cards all over the refrigerator and won't let me get rid of even one of them. They think you are pretty special traveling around like your Dad did in the service. He is glad you got work on cars out there.

That girl Regina you traveled with to Ohio, the one who used to waitress down at the restaurant where your Dad and I like to go, came back here. She is learning to drive a truck! Her uncle is that big trucking man Jack Tonneau. Are you still friends? Your Dad says since you're in with the Tonneaus maybe you can get them to throw some business his way for the garage.

It is still dead of winter here, the groundhog never even poked his head out this year. I guess if you've got orange trees you are warm.

Love, Ma

She read the part about Regina again, cold with shock. And again, until Clover whimpered to go walking. Then she scrubbed the garage dirt off herself until she was shiny.

All this chasing after Regina to have her turn around and go back home. She was driving trucks like Jody. Her pretty Regina.

Was this one of those times when she should just say no? Say the heck with Regina, life was better without her? Things sure didn't get any easier just because she'd found out that she had the right to say no.

She was numb as she walked over to meet Jas. The palm trees and the flowers had disappeared. She had to remind herself to stop looking for Regina out of the corner of her eye.

It was a relief to see Jas, smiling and ready to play. Andy really had forgotten, after one night, the joy of her fresh-faced prettiness. At that moment she wanted nothing but to keep this pleasant, smiling woman in her sight always. What, though, did she have to offer Jas? Regina hadn't found enough to stay.

"Clover!" Jas greeted the dog like a long-lost friend. "I've heard so much about you! You look like the pup I grew up with, Puddles." Clover tried to lick her glasses, but Jas flipped her over and rubbed her tummy. "The name was from her brown spots, not any accidents she had," she explained.

"Sure," teased Andy.

They set off down Twentieth Street. "I have so much to show you!" Jas said.

Regina dogged their steps. Instead of asking about the flowers Andy found herself saying, "I have to tell you what I got in the mail."

Jas stopped, a look of concern echoing the worry in Andy's voice. "You heard from *her*."

"No. But Ma wrote that she's back home."

Jas was silent, tracing a Y-shaped crack in the sidewalk with the toe of her running shoe. "You're going back?"

"I think it hasn't had time to sink in yet. I mean, what's she doing there? Why's she driving a truck? It was hard enough being gay in town together, what's she going to do alone?"

Jas moved to a little yellow car and leaned against it. "You haven't told me much about her, but I can't believe any woman in her right mind would leave you."

"Sometimes I don't think she is in her right mind."

The city creaked and wheezed and roared around them. Jas looked so fresh, like one of the spring

184

flowers, and so trusting, leaning against that car, thinking hard to help her.

She took Jas's hand and tugged Clover's leash. "Come on," she said. "You promised us a walk."

"I wanted to show you Mission Street. It's totally cool."

It was a crowded jangling street just going neon in the twilight, as if the fine Banbury Cross lady were putting on her rings and bells, getting ready for the night. They went into the Rainbow Grocery where they filled a basket with goodies.

"We'd better eat the ice cream first," said Jas.

"We can't eat dessert before dinner!"

"It'll melt if we don't."

She felt like a kid, licking vanilla ice cream off a wooden spoon. Clover cleaned out both cups. They passed dozens of little shops whose signs, more often than not, were in Spanish rather than English. Women and children, old men and young, thronged the streets and everywhere bargains were offered.

At a subway stop men lounged on benches, teenage boys watched young women, commuters were streaming up the stairs. The street lights came on just before dark. Why did this town feel more festive than New York, safer?

"You've been to the women's bar; now you've got to see the Rawhide," said Jas. They walked back to Andy's and left Clover there, then caught a bus in the night.

When they arrived a show was going on. "Those are the Saddle Tramps," whispered Jas. Her eyes shone with excitement.

In black pants and gray Western shirts, twelve

couples, men and women mixed every which way, swung and pranced to the country music.

"I've never seen gay people square-dance," she whispered back.

"It's not exactly square-dancing."

"Well, all-American stuff in costumes. My folks used to go out once in a while over to the Grange." She felt moved to tears. "We really are just like regular people."

Jas looked at her. "Yes. We're regular and special."

The Saddle Tramps left the floor to spirited applause. Jas taught her the basic two-step. They swung around the floor in circles for a while then and she didn't wonder about Regina until they were off the bus and nearing Jas's apartment.

"Do you still think about your ex?"

Jas frowned. "Not too much any more. It's been six months. It's like the whole thing is light years away," Jas said, looking right into her eyes. "Do you think you might go back to New Hampshire?"

She reached for Jas's hand, then pulled back, feeling like she had no right to it.

"Gimme," said Jas.

Jas's hand felt small and soft. Her hair was like feathers around her face. I could treasure this woman, Andy thought, every bit as much as Regina.

"Look at you!" she said in Jas's kitchen. "You're *so* pretty!"

Jas pulled back. "Don't be silly. That's the last thing I am."

"But you are."

Jas pursed her lips. "I know it's dark outside,

but before I make tea I want to show you my garden."

"Here? On the third floor?"

"Some of it. I like the challenge."

They stepped over Jas's white nurse shoes and went out the back door. Jas switched on the porch light. The night was cool and moist. The porch was a maze of planters.

"I'm glad you think I'm pretty, but pretty is a loaded word for me," said Jas. Her voice was quiet, stubborn. "My mother liked everything so *pretty.* Pretty, pretty, pretty, all the time. Her flower garden, our life, my name, *me.*" She was watering her pots with a hose, carefully, as if she could measure the moisture. "I disappointed her there."

"Is that why you think you're not pretty?"

"Not like she wanted me to be. Not beauty-contest pretty, and that was the only kind for her. She never forgave me for needing glasses and you would have thought it was my fault that contacts gave me eye infections. We tried every doctor in Burlington, but I just couldn't wear them." The stubborn tone became bitter. "I have friends who tell me the way I feel about my mother is an unresolved issue for me and maybe it is, but I'm as disappointed in her as she is in me."

She sprayed water into a garbage can. Andy was amazed to see that it was filled with soil and green shoots were pushing up.

"You know what I think is pretty? These potatoes growing so far down in the dark earth. Peas growing up their vines. Carrot tops all lacy and delicate-looking. I may not be a beauty, but I'm practical. And porch gardening is fun. My mother used to curse the gophers when they'd get her flowers. All I have to worry about up here are the pussycats who think I'm the goddess of kitty potties and go digging up my sprouts." Jas showed her the screens she used to keep the cats out.

As they made their way down three flights of wooden steps to the yard, they passed the shallower bins of onions and garlic.

"The owner doesn't live here and the other tenants only use the yard for tanning. I've got this whole back plot. Everything's organic. Down here I have to chase the raccoons as well as the cats."

Jas walked the garden, pointing out phantom lettuce, cucumbers, corn and beans. "Here's my little herb garden. Mustard, oregano, basil, mint, and some others. And these," she pointed to the back fence, covered with tall shrubs, "are my jasmines. It's what I did to help me learn who I am. I'll bet you never knew how many kinds of jasmines there are. I've planted American jasmine, which is really red morning glory, and sweet jasmine, the one used in tea. Red jasmine is a natural perfume, and this one's false jasmine, my favorite. It's yellow — my mother wanted me to be blonde like her. The fragrance is wonderful."

"The garden is your Studebaker."

They beamed at each other.

"Let me make the tea or I'll never get up in the morning."

When they were seated at Jas's old wooden table she asked Andy, "So are you going back East?"

"I guess I haven't had a chance to think about Regina being there. I like it here. I can't understand why anyone lives in that cold, with no work, and no gay people, and relatives breathing down their necks. But I came here to find Regina. And that old Studebaker. Once I get my car back, I won't have any idea what to do."

"Maybe you can go looking for Andy too," Jas said.

"Why does everybody say that?"

Jas's face changed. "I'm sorry. I don't mean to be a know-it-all. You just sound so obsessed with getting these pieces of your life back that are outside you. It took losing my relationship to figure out that all I really need is me. The rest is frosting on the cake."

"But how do you learn these things?"

Jas fingered her earthenware mug. "There's something about all the hurting I did that left space in my head. It's like the pain burnt holes in my mind and the scars that formed were made out of odds and ends of wisdom."

"I've been through the pain, but how do I know if I learned anything?"

"Talking to people."

"Nobody wants to hear about my problems."

"I had somewhere to go. When I was a kid I enjoyed the walks to the old white church, seeing the other families in their best clothes. Then I went to nursing school, came out, and forgot all about God. I think this last lover became my Goddess. After the breakup I went to the Parsonage on Castro Street, which is for gay people. They're easy to talk to and they've all been through it, just like me." Jas looked into her eyes. "I have friends I won't give up no matter who I'm seeing. Lovers go away. Friends don't. I want a friend who'll also be my lover."

* * * * *

On the day of the car fair they packed lunches and Nicholas drove Jasmine, Andy and Clover to the huge field where proud collectors wiped the last of the morning fog off their Packards and 1943 Buicks, their tail-finned Oldsmobiles and hunched Hudsons. They saw Old Johnny the pump jockey inspecting Karmann Ghias. He let Andy tell him about that old Studebaker.

"If she's in that good shape she's probably not parts yet, but neither is anybody going to show her someplace this open. Let me ask around to see what I can pick up."

Andy took a picture of Jas and Clover in front of a yellow 1949 Nash Airflyte, something like the one she'd driven in college.

The Studebakers were next to the Packards, with some Studebaker-Packards in between. She was looking around for the right one to put in a picture when she saw that old Studebaker. Her heart felt like it would jump out of her chest.

Nicholas saw the look on her face. "Whoa, girl. It's probably just a look-alike."

"No, it's not."

"Shut up, Andy. Keep a low profile till we can check it out for sure."

Hands fisted in her pockets, taking deep breaths to keep from crying, Andy strolled between her friends as they pretended interest in other cars. The crowd was thin here, but still they had to wait to look inside until two men moved on.

"You're right. That's not it," said Andy, spitting into the grass.

"I hate when you do that," Jasmine said.

190

Andy jumped.

"It's not very constructive," Jas explained. "Like a cat scratching at linoleum to cover up food it doesn't like."

"All right," she answered brusquely, hot with embarrassment and fear that she'd drive Jas away.

The man displaying the Studebaker sat on a lawn chair smoking a cigar. The men who'd been looking inside stood with him.

Andy started to explain about the spitting.

"Quiet. He's telling them about one he's got somewhere else," Jas, who stood closest to the men, said.

"What kind? Where?"

"Shh. He's giving them the address to go look at it."

"There they go," said Nicholas, "toward the lot. Let's get my truck."

"Slow down, damn it!" Andy told them gruffly. They were so obvious, huge Nicholas and old Johnny who spat tobacco like a character actor in a Western. There was no way she could just let things happen. It was her car. She was taking charge of her life.

"Take it easy, Andy," Jas said, taking her hand.

She dropped Jas's hand as if it burned. "We don't want people noticing us now! It's bad enough with Old Johnny gimping along at a hundred miles an hour, and Nicholas's damned yellow hat. Stop pulling, Clover!" she whispered with a harsh tug at her leash.

Jas moved away from her, silent. They hurried into the bed of Nicholas' pickup.

Didn't Jas understand how important the

191

Studebaker was to her? If she didn't get it back, what good was living?

"The thing is," Andy shouted over the noise of the truck, "is that I'm trying to have some say-so in my life. It looks like I'm doing everything all wrong, though."

"What," asked Jasmine, "did any of us do perfectly on the first try?"

"Oh. Like, if at first you don't succeed." She shook her head, smiling. "I'll worry about that later. Let's see if this is my car."

"If it'll calm you down, then I hope so. And I know enough not to get between a woman and her car," Jas said with one of her teasing smiles, head tilted sideways.

They followed the men from the car fair halfway back to San Francisco, to a wrecking yard just off the freeway. The buyers went into the office and came right out. They didn't get into their car, but went through an opening in the tall chain-link fence, after a glance behind them.

Old Johnny and Nicholas came around to the back of the pickup. "Devil's Pit," said Old Johnny.

"It's a legitimate business up front," Nicholas explained, "but out back it's a mine field of stolen cars and parts and drugs. They make so much money their fancy lawyer just dances around the cops when they make a bust. It's called Devil's Pit because if something or someone goes in there it doesn't come back out in recognizable form."

"No!" she said in a small voice. Jas squeezed her hand.

Old Johnny said, "But you said you have a key, if that's your car in there."

"What good will that do me?"

Old Johnny looked at Nicholas. "I thought you only took on smart partners."

"He means we ought to steal it back, Andy."

"Oh, Nicholas," Jas chided.

"Gals, it's the only way to do business with these crooks," Old Johnny advised. "What can they do, call the boys in blue?"

"Just take it?"

"Here they come," warned Jas.

"What should I do?"

"I'll tell you, if we catch up with it, you might want to keep the car under wraps a few weeks, just so no one steals it back or takes a baseball bat to it. The Devil's Pit mob'll probably think those two fellas took it if nobody makes them wiser." He laughed. "Those poor rubes. How about a long drive home to New Hampshire?"

She looked at Jasmine in panic. Is this the way it would work out then?"

"What are you trying to do, chase off my new partner here?" Nicholas asked.

"I'm so nervous I don't even know if I could drive it."

Jas's concerned look scared her even more despite her reassuring words. "You'll do fine, Andy, and we'll all be with you."

"No, not for this part of it. If I get caught in there I don't want any of you getting in trouble too. I'm going in alone." She felt like Clint Eastwood and rolled up her sleeves.

"Then we'll be ready to follow you in the truck," promised Nicholas.

"Or," said Old Johnny, "to put you back together again if —"

"I'm no Humpty Dumpty and I'm not going through this again. It's my Studebaker. I'm just saying no to those stupid car thieves and these creeps who think that old Studebaker is a hunk of scrap they can steal and sell." Her anger burned smooth and made her feel strong.

She passed Clover's leash to Jas, and with a deep breath turned and crossed the road. She walked along the fence a while, then, sure no one had noticed her, ducked through it.

"Please Goddess, if you'll give me back my car I won't ask for anything more," she prayed silently. "Except Regina. I know that's a lot to ask, but what good is the car without —"

Something moved to her left. Her heart thudded and she felt dizzy, but she kept right on going as if she belonged there.

"Okay, okay, Goddess. Life's good even without Regina."

No one challenged her as she walked swiftly back, back, back through the heaps of junked cars, the piles of scrap, of half-sorted headlights, bumpers, hoods. Then she saw the row of older cars. Some needed body work, but that old Studebaker shone like it had never crossed the desert. Without even a cursory examination she slid behind the wheel. The smell was right, the floor mats were the ones she'd bought back home, red with the crowns in the middle. And miracle of miracles, the key turned and the spark of life was there.

"My good old car," she said, and was off. She locked the doors as she drove, allowing herself one moment of elation before she took another deep breath and turned the corner by the office.

"Oh my gosh. Oh my gosh. Oh my gosh," Andy chanted as she approached the building. She could see people moving inside. Then she was out the gate, holding herself back from screeching away. Nicholas's truck came hurtling behind her, to shield her from view.

CHAPTER NINETEEN

Less than two hours later Nicholas slammed the garage door shut. "We did it!" he yelled. Old Johnny was pumping Andy's hand so hard her teeth rattled. Or maybe it wasn't from the handshake — she was shaking all over. She ran her fingers along the Studebaker's body and over the dash. She looked under the hood, then wiped off some dust. Her fingers felt the tiny dents made by Windy's shotgun, but otherwise there was no damage.

Jas, who insisted on a congratulatory hug, smelled fresh and clean, felt warm and soft. Andy's breath grew short, and she was a little dizzy and giddy as she stepped away from Jas, saying, "I want to take you all out to celebrate, right now."

"Johnny," asked Nicholas, laughing, "have you ever been in a gay bar before?"

"What do you mean? What do you want with one of those?" He looked puzzled and waited for an answer from Nicholas. Then his face changed, his eyes narrowed in anger. "You're not telling me I've been riding around with a bunch of homos, are you?"

He stared at them, one after the other. Andy felt deflated, like a balloon about to slide onto the floor.

"Gays, Johnny. I thought you knew." Nicholas looked like his heart would break.

Old Johnny spat on the garage floor, turned and left.

Silence filled the garage. "So much for self-outing," Nicholas said, his voice sad.

"Straights always assume we're like them unless we're carrying on in front of them," said Jas, her voice disgusted.

"Well, he got my car back."

"But can you keep it now? I think we need to look for a hiding place Old Johnny doesn't know," said Nicholas, slumping onto the folding chair he kept for customers.

"This is San Francisco, nineteen ninety!" exclaimed Jas. "I came here to get *away* from that homophobic crap."

Nicholas picked up a piece of chamois cloth and began to rub the Studebaker. "This may be the city of Harvey Milk's victory, but it's also the city where he was murdered." He stood. "I think I'll stick around and finish up some work."

197

"Are you worried Old Johnny'll come back?"

"I'm hoping he'll come back and apologize."

"You know the antidote," said Jas.

Nicholas looked at her, his basset face drooping.

"The gay pride parade. I've been meaning to talk to you about marching in it this year. How could we get to ride in Andy's car and have the whole city welcome her?"

The crescent smile appeared, complete with gold dog teeth. Even his ears rose when he smiled. "Let me think about it. I'll bet we can come up with something. This is, after all, a gay business we have here." He put a tape on.

"What a great advertisement the Studebaker would make for you," said Jas.

"I wonder if it's time for the business to surface and turn legit. In the spirit of gay pride, of coming out. I could rename it to show there's a lesbian involved," Nicholas mused. "How about the Queer Musketeers!"

Jas groaned.

"I like it!" said Andy. She pictured herself driving the Studebaker under that banner as if she'd lived in San Francisco all her life and really belonged. What would it feel like to know the whole world was watching you be queer? Maybe Regina would see her and want her back, she'd be so proud.

No, darn it. She didn't need to be doing anything for Regina any more. Maybe it would lift her own spirits and get rid of that hounded feeling she had because she was gay. It was insurance against turning out like Jody the trucker.

The city was clouded over. She walked in silence with Jas and Clover straight up Twentieth, climbed

Collingwood to the stairs and sat overlooking Twenty-second and Diamond. It was a quiet neighborhood with cats sitting in the windows of one of every three houses along the block. Someone had painted green, white and black stripes on the house to their right so it looked like a piece of that Pop Art she'd seen in the museums in Chicago. Twin Peaks rose before them, its red and white radio towers for once not shrouded by fog.

"I don't like cities, and I really miss seeing all the stars at night, but maybe this is why San Francisco feels like home," she said.

"Why?" Jas asked, braiding Clover's tail fur.

"The hills. We have real good hills in Weirs Beach. Regina's folks own one of the guest houses on the steepest hill. She's probably staying there now. It's off season. There might be some ice fishing out on the lake, but it's getting kind of late for that."

"Not on Champlain. She's still frozen solid sometimes in April."

"Do you miss it?"

Jas laughed. She used a piece of string she'd found in her pocket to tie a bow on Clover's braid. "Doggie punk," she said. "I know I'm supposed to miss the seasons, the colors in the fall, McIntosh apples and white church steeples, but I wouldn't take all that over San Francisco any day." She pointed to the city. "It's like a magical kingdom here. Fairytale houses, an enchanted Bay, princesses and princes on every block. Even the food is insane. Did you ever taste riper fruit?"

"Don't you remember those strawberries the second or third time we walked, Jasmine Jones?"

"You mean the ones you thought were sweetened?

Why do you think I wore my strawberry dress today, Andy Blaine?"

"For me?"

Jas nodded and was silent for a while. "I feel nostalgic about Vermont," she said finally, "but no, I don't miss it." Anxiety clouded Jas's eyes again.

"I don't really want to go back either," said Andy, filling the silence. "Maybe for a visit. I'd love to see where you grew up, and show you where I did. I just think I ought to go now, though, to finish what I started."

"Regina?"

"If you love somebody you stay with her."

"I agree, but not if she doesn't stay with you. Not if she hasn't once tried to get in touch with you. It works both ways, you know."

There was a strain in Jas's voice that sounded like pleading. It scared Andy a little, as if Jas might need too much, or at least more than Andy thought she could give.

"I guess you want me to stay."

Jas started a tiny braid at the tip of Clover's tail. "Of course I do." Her lower lip protruded as she spoke, as if she were trying to hold back tears. "I've fallen in love with you, Andy Blaine. But I don't want only half of Andy to stay." Now the tears came. "If you really belong with Regina I'd rather know it now."

Andy didn't know what to say. Did she love them both?

Jas dried her eyes, blew her nose and smoothed her hair. "I love how fresh you are, Andy, but you have to be a little harder to protect yourself, protect whatever you have that means anything to you."

Taking a deep breath, Jas said, "I hate like anything to suggest this, but I have to know, too. Why don't you just call her?"

"Call Regina?" She stared at Jas. Regina wasn't at an unofficial lesbian inn or on women's land with no listing in the book. Andy didn't have to hope that someone else would have the number. Regina's folks would be listed with Information.

"Sure. Scope out the territory. It's easier than driving three thousand miles."

Call Regina. Talk to her today, in a few minutes. Talk to her folks, her sister, her brother. Talk to her in Weirs Beach. Andy's hands felt frozen. There was a chilly sweat on her forehead. Her mouth was bone dry. Twenty-second Street turned all fuzzy before her eyes.

She tried it on every way she could think of. She might not be home. It was Sunday evening there, though, so she probably would be. Unless. "Oh God, she's probably down at the arcades playing Pacman with Roy or somebody."

If only there were someone back in Weirs Beach she was close to. If only Gramma weren't dead. It seemed like a lifetime ago that she'd died, but, Andy realized, she wouldn't even be seventy if she were still alive. She would have known everything that was happening in town.

Jas was talking. "She may be home pining for you."

"You think so? No, you don't really think so at all. Come on. Let's find a phone."

They walked downhill until they found a booth. Jas gave her a credit card. "This is an investment in my future too," she said as she took Clover.

201

Andy watched until they were at the other end of the block, then followed the instructions on the phone. Her hands shook so badly she could barely punch the buttons. She got the number from Information with no trouble. She was so nervous that on her first try a computer broke in to tell her she hadn't dialed an area code. She tried again. While she waited, a picture of Gramma in the casket came back to her. She didn't want to remember her that way.

This time the computer told her the circuits were busy. She dialed again, remembering the whole family drinking and eating and even laughing after the funeral. She'd wanted to tell them all to shut up and get out. How could she cry in front of everybody?

A recording told her that the number was disconnected, but she realized she'd gotten confused again and dialed her own area code. Sweating everywhere now, she called the operator and asked for help, but the operator got a busy signal. She listened to it bleep on and on. Wasn't there any way she could get through? It'd been awful when they showed her Everett in a crib. The crib was white like the casket and she'd shrieked in fear. He'd looked as strange as Gramma, and Andy had started screaming the way she'd wanted Gramma to, to protest death. She didn't want anything to do with him. How dare that wrinkly red rodent come to take Gramma's place.

By this time she was almost in tears, paralyzed in the phone booth. She remembered the Studebaker, and poor Nicholas in there with it, probably being tortured by car thieves. Her folks had given her little brother Gramma's room, because there'd have to be a boys' room. She'd cried night after night, hardly ate anything. Ma took her to the baby doctor. He gave her a bottle of tonic that tasted like iodine, beets and lamb grease and she threw it up every time they forced it down her throat. It was her life, she didn't have to live it.

Clover and Jas came into sight two blocks up, heading back. She banished thoughts of Gramma and told herself, *Andy, you're being a big baby.* Breathing deeply, she imagined a stream of white light coming out of the heavens and surrounding her. She very slowly and deliberately punched buttons on the phone.

"Hello?"

It was Regina's mother.

"Hello?" repeated Mrs. Tonneau. She couldn't get any words out. "Is anyone there?"

"Is — is Regina there?"

"Regina? Just a minute. Who's calling?"

"It's —" she closed her eyes very tightly and felt her index finger depress the cradle. "It's Andy," she whispered into the San Francisco air. "It's Andy," she said into the warm sweet sunshine.

By the time Jas got to the booth Andy was crying without restraint. Jas put her arms around her and held her. "I'm sorry," she told Jas. "I can't stop."

"It's okay. Let it out. Cry like you're the heavens in a summer storm."

Clover looked up at her with head cocked.

"Oh my dog," she said, kneeling down and wrapping her arms around the shaggy fur. She stretched one hand to Jas. "My dog, my friend." She sobbed, choked, coughed, wiped her eyes with a sleeve. "My car too, we have my car back. And I have a job, and a nice room."

"You have a lot. You certainly have my friendship. And Nicholas's. And probably Cricket's and Umeko's and Meg's."

"Oh, Jas, it hurts."

"I know, baby. I know. It won't hurt forever, that's the only comfort I can give you."

"But it has hurt forever!"

"Tell me what she said."

"What she said? She didn't say anything! Her mom said she was home, but I hung up. I didn't want to talk to her." Jas stroked her hair. "I didn't want to talk to Regina. I loved her ten minutes ago. What happened?"

"You didn't want to be hurt any more."

"But I loved her so much. I really believed in us. I believed she wanted us."

"Poor Andy."

"Didn't she believe? Didn't she ever want us too?"

"It's all right."

"Regina! Why did you leave? What's wrong with me?" she shouted, standing. "How *could* you, Gramma?" She was enraged and kicked the phone booth.

"What does Gramma have to do with it?" Jas asked.

"Ouch! Shit. How could Regina dance with all those men and sleep with other women and then take off on me and never call my folks to see where I am? How could she just forget how we danced? Is she a faucet, just shutting off how she feels? She's crazy!"

"She may be, or she may be like my ex, just different than when you met."

"But I would have stayed with her through anything! I loved her! And now I don't even have the love left. I don't even love her anymore. Damn her, damn her, damn her, damn her."

She couldn't stand up. Jas supported her.

"I don't want to talk to her, I don't want to see her, I just want to love her!"

"Andy, come on. Let's go back to your room."

"Why? Am I acting like a big baby?"

Jas didn't answer. That brought her out of it. She swallowed air until the sobbing stopped, then she mopped up her face. "I'm going to call her back. I can't just drop it."

"I love how you're fighting to keep what you had, but you've been through enough for today. Sleep on it."

With a long sigh Andy agreed.

Meg let her put the Studebaker in her garage at the inn. Jas had made plans to spend Sunday with other friends and Nicholas was at the beach with an out-of-town lover. Andy didn't dare drive the Studebaker, but she brought some tools over from the garage and tuned it up. It'd been run hard, but not damaged. Later, she took Clover to Glen Canyon Park for a long run.

She found a phone booth.

"Starr? It's Andy." She told him everything.

"Well, call Regina, hon. You're obviously not going to be satisfied till you get it from the horse's mouth. But if I were you, now that you have your chariot back, I'd take on that lovely new babe you've been courting. Jasmine Jones — nice moniker."

"I'm not courting her."

"Someday you'll open your eyes and discover you're as real as the rest of us, sweetie, whether you want to be or not. Regina may turn out whole and healed and sweet as banana cream pie, which, by the way, we're having for dessert tonight, eat your heart out. But regardless of who Regina finally is, you deserve to live your own life. Now. And she's removed herself. You've got to say no to the past and yes to Andy."

There it was again. It sounded so simple: Just say no.

She spent another forty-five minutes throwing a stick for Clover. When it was totally pulverized, they headed home. Every time they passed a phone, Andy would silently rehearse her call to Regina, then pass by. She'd never realized there were that many phone booths in the world. When she spotted a phone booth under a palm tree she knew she had no choice. She might as well jump over her candlestick. It wasn't going to get any better.

"This is Andy Blaine," she told Mrs. Tonneau. She wondered if word had gotten as far as their parents about her and Regina being queer.

"The redhead? I remember you. You just missed Regina. She was back for a couple of months, learning to wheel those big trucks my brother-in-law has. She's a fast learner, got her license two days ago and left late last night. You in town? Doesn't sound like it."

If Mrs. Tonneau knew about them she wasn't letting on. "I'm in San Francisco, California."

"Aren't you kids the travelers. Maybe she'll get sent out that way. She's buying the truck from Jack as she goes. He set her up with a broker. You want to leave your number?"

Darn, she didn't know the number at the inn yet. She couldn't give her Jas's number and she didn't have the one at the garage memorized. "I can leave you my addresses at home and where I work. W-w-will she call you?"

"Said she would."

And that was that. Maybe she'd hear from Regina, maybe she wouldn't. She was willing to join the crowd that thought she wouldn't and get on with her life.

The Studebaker stayed hidden for three weeks. Nicholas kept in touch with contacts other than Old Johnny, who never had come back, and there seemed to be no dragnet out looking for the car. To be completely legitimate, Andy reported recovery of her stolen car to the Arizona police. Life became calm, full of the little joys and frustrations Andy hadn't enjoyed since she was on her own in New Hampshire.

On the fourth Saturday after the Studebaker's rescue she cruised along Twenty-fourth, basking in the feel of driving again. Jas was to be outside Bell's Market waiting but all Andy saw were two men drinking from a paper bag, a woman in an enormous sun hat, and some kids on skateboards. Then she saw that the woman wore a strawberry print sundress and had a picnic basket at her feet. It was Jas.

She pulled up, leapt out of the car and ran around to take the basket, and opened the passenger door. Jas smiled and gracefully accepted these favors.

"You look terrific!" said Andy.

"Thank you." Jas tucked her skirt under her as she sat.

"Like a real lady."

Jas peered over her sunglasses. "I'm not at all sure it's really ladyness I was after. Just some kind of style. You do butch like you were born to it."

Andy headed the Studebaker toward Golden Gate Park, feeling a little uneasy about her excitement. One of the things she liked about Jas was her predictability. She didn't know this dress-up side of her.

"You're wearing makeup!"

"Do you mind?"

She swallowed hard. What was she feeling? Excitement? Fear? Or both? "No. You look beautiful. I love it."

Even Jas's smile was different. Was it just the lipstick? Was it the fact that Jas was sitting — oh, no! — in Regina's seat? That she hadn't opened a door for a woman since Willa? That she hadn't felt this want in her gut since Regina? Her excitement gushed onto her underwear.

She flubbed parking she was so nervous. Back and forth she went, trying to put that old Studebaker into a large parking space.

"I'm sorry," she said when they were finally in and the line of cars that had formed behind her passed, staring at this incompetent woman driver.

"Sorry that I'm flustering you? I kind of like it."

Was Jas coming on to her?

She ran around to open the door, carefully locked both sides and rolled the windows tight, then carried the basket into the park. Jas slipped a hand under her forearm. She stole glances at Jas, marveling at her transformation under the hat and makeup.

"You did something to your hair, too."

"It's just hidden."

Jas had a long slender neck. Andy imagined running her lips along it.

Early for picnicking, they got a wonderful tree on Stow Lake, where she could still keep an eye on the car. An old Army blanket had been stashed in the Studebaker since New Hampshire. Jas settled on it, kicking off her sandals, gracefully arranging the dress around herself. The grass smelled sweet where they'd stepped on it. There was a hush over the park as if even the wind had been banished and everything in the world was waiting, waiting for Andy to —

She was tongue-tied. A long-term blush took over her face. She fiddled in her pocket with her pomegranate seeds. She sat several feet from Jas. Clover wasn't even here to help. Jas had asked for a day by themselves so Andy'd let Nicholas take the dog along with him to the beach. As a matter of fact, she almost wished she'd gone with Nicholas herself. Jas looked like a movie star. How was Andy supposed to act?

What had Starr advised? Had she really been courting Jas? Had she started something she couldn't finish?

Andy stopped tugging at the grass and took a deep breath. This was like the first dance with Regina. The first day Willa took her shirt off in the motel. Uh-oh, she thought, is this going to be another first time? But then, what was wrong with that? Jasmine Jones was a beautiful woman. She wanted Jas. What was there to get unglued about?

Her hands trembled as she poured lemonade from the thermos. "Nice day," she said.

Jas graciously agreed.

"How was the hospital yesterday?" Normally, Jas would tell some funny story about a patient or co-worker.

"Pretty quiet. The usual." Pause. Long silence. "How was the garage?"

She felt like a total geek.

When Jas suggested that they eat, Andy pounced on the idea of food, but it only got worse. Jas set out a fancy spread, including tiny sandwiches and linen napkins that had been her grandmother's.

Andy felt like a bear that had blundered into a picnic. Wasn't there a pill that would transform her into Cary Grant?

She took three deep breaths, looked to the road to make sure the Studebaker was okay, then squirmed over next to Jas against the tree, praying for white light.

"You sure look pretty. Is that nail polish?"

Jas held out a hand which only had looked useful before today. It was glamorous. Andy felt the smooth nails with her fingertips. Jas leaned into her shoulder, refusing to make the first move. Was this the day Starr predicted? The day she'd have to keep her eyes open and be as real as everyone else? She had to, right then, decide whether or not she was gay.

Gramma came to the rescue. Andy remembered every word and she got on her knees to recite:

"Curlylocks, Curlylocks,/Wilt thou be mine?/Thou shalt not wash dishes/Nor feed the swine,/But sit on a cushion/And sew a fine seam,/And feed upon strawberries,/Sugar and cream."

Suddenly it was easy. With an arm around Jas she drew her closer. Jas's head tipped back and she was kissing that long throat, all the way up under the earlobes and then, her lips.

Jas had removed her sunglasses. Her smoky eyes opened, wide and loving, but she was shaking. Andy kissed her again, tasting Jas's candy-like lipstick, and relaxed into the kiss, as she would into a favorite feather pillow, or a bed rich with soft covers. What a wonderful way to wake up.

They shifted, front to front. The sun hat fell back and she felt in Jas's shaking her frailty, as well as the firm stuff she was made of. Leaning on her hands, she pressed her breasts against Jas's breasts, rubbed sideways. Jas let out a kittenish sound. This was a gift, this lovely woman underneath her.

She kissed Jas again, ran her tongue along the outline of her lips, pushed in, felt her teeth, pushed farther and found her tongue. "Oh, Jas," she said, pulling away, lying on her side, loving Jas's face with her hand. This felt like a sacred rite, an exchange of silent vows despite all the risk and fear.

"I'll love you," she said, eyes on Jasmine's eyes, "the best I can. I'll treasure you. You're as precious as all the little animals and the trees. You're exactly who I want." And, she thought with Regina whispering unkind things in her head, you're nice to me.

Tenderly, she lay Jas down again and held her close, kissing all around the edges of her hairline.

211

"Andy, I love you," said Jas, hands gentle at her back.

She felt safe, cherished in Jas's arms. It felt so good. Gramma would approve.

Gramma. She hadn't felt this good since she was seven and had Gramma. Had she gotten her dander up so badly back when Gramma died that she'd quit life as much as she could?

"I love you, Jasmine Jones," she whispered.

Jas seemed to kiss her forever, with sweet short kisses and smiles between each flurry. Faintly Jas answered, "I want to make love to you, Andy. Take me home."

They only napped that night.

CHAPTER TWENTY

"You look like the Cheshire cat," said Nicholas.

It was Monday morning at the garage. Andy's grin felt like hot butterscotch sauce dripping off her lips. It grew even bigger when it occurred to her that that was pretty much what Jas tasted like all over. Butterscotch always had been her favorite flavor.

"Jasmine Jones?" asked Nicholas.

She felt the wildest hottest blush of her life suffuse her whole body, and she nodded.

"It's about time," Nicholas said, his gold teeth like stars across the garage.

"How was the beach?"

"Balmy."

"Thanks for keeping Clover overnight."

"It would've been nice if you'd let me in on why you called. I thought maybe you were holding the Studebaker Gang at bay outside your door."

"No. I wasn't holding off anybody last night." They laughed.

Andy hummed inside with well-being. Their three-day anniversary would be today and she'd been imagining what color flowers she'd bring to Jas. She wanted to celebrate constantly the confidence she felt for the first time in her life. And to celebrate being gay. What a mega-mistake that would have been, running back home where she would have slammed the closet door shut forever on Jas. Nursery rhymes, those dire foreboding guideposts, seemed to go off less often in her head as she dared to take hold of her life by the horns. She'd stuck the snapshot over her bed at the inn to remind herself of Andy/Babe the Blue Ox.

An hour later, Nicholas came out from underneath an old T-Bird. "I guess you're settling in San Francisco."

"You do?"

"You've got a woman, a job, a place to hang your hat."

"But I like traveling."

"Just tell me when you want to take off — as long as you come back."

"I need to see the Grand Canyon, and the Redwoods, and the Oregon Coast. I've never seen the

South or New Orleans. I want to go to Canada and Mexico. And Alaska! And go home with Jas and bring her to see where I grew up."

"Sounds like you should have been the truck driver, not Regina. Hey, what about Regina anyway? She write yet?"

"No."

"It'd be nice to get that closed, wouldn't it?"

"Maybe I can just forget her now."

Nicholas raised his eyebrows. "You're still wet behind the ears, aren't you, Andy? We never forget any of them, not one."

She'd just drained the oil from a VW when there was a rumbling outside. They stood stock still.

"Shit," said Nicholas. "Not another earthquake." The sound ended. "Only about a two."

They went back to work. Nicholas turned up the opera. The rumbling returned.

"Maybe it's a truck. Don't tell me those parts got shipped here right from the wholesaler."

Nicholas rolled up the garage door. A huge semi was parked on Chattanooga. The driver must have gone by once before looking for the address. Disappearing around to the driver's side, Nicholas yelled back, "I'll tell him to park around the corner. Keep the neighbors happy."

She yanked some dirty spark plugs from the old VW and wiped them clean, trying to decide if they could be saved. Why didn't people keep their cars in better shape? It made her angry to see a car neglected. The owners should be grateful they had wheels. But then, maybe all these people who were ignorant of cars knew more about life than she did. All she knew was cars.

215

"Uh, Andy?" Nicholas stood beside her.

"Look at these plugs. I bet this guy didn't even get them checked under warranty."

"I don't know how to tell you this, Andy, but you have a visitor.

She followed Nicholas' gaze.

"Regina," she said, suddenly cold to the bone.

Andy stood silent, frozen with conflicting emotions. The face she loved was back before her, but all she felt was pain. How could it be that a sight that had given her so much pleasure made her feel like a car in a head-on collision?

Regina licked her lips. In her gold-green eyes, as always, were warring camps — a smile mixed with apprehension. Her head tipped to one side as if questioning. Her hands were still, but her arms were just slightly raised as if she hoped for an embrace.

"You're much thinner," Regina said. She wore designer jeans, baby blue leather high-tops and a pink turtleneck jersey under a white sweatshirt. The sweatshirt showed the Mt. Washington steaming across Lake Winnepesaukee.

I love you, Andy wanted to blurt, but her mouth wouldn't open for those words. "Your hair is shorter."

"It's easier to take care of on the road this way."

I hate you, she wanted to say, but that wouldn't come out either.

"Want to go for a ride?" asked Regina.

"I'm mad at you," she answered, then stepped back, not believing she'd let it escape. Nicholas slipped outside.

Regina didn't respond right away. The apprehension in her eyes turned to hurt, but the smile remained. She was silent.

Andy forced herself to think. What was she feeling? Then she forced herself to say the words. "I wanted to be with you forever. You told me that's what you wanted too, but that's not how you acted."

Regina just lowered her head.

"How could you do that, Regina?" she asked through gritted teeth, trying not to cry. She shook with the fear of speaking her anger. She felt like lightning would come from the sky and knock her dead.

"I don't know, Andy. It's where I was at then."

There was pain in Regina's face. Andy wanted to take her in her arms and soothe her, but Regina was fire and would burn her. So she just cried and asked, "Why, why why?" unable to finish any more sentences. *Why did you leave? Why did you want the others? Why are you here? What do you want?*

"I thought we could talk," said Regina. "That you'd be proud of what I've done for myself. But you're too mad. Maybe I'll stop by again next trip." She turned and walked out of the garage, then stopped for a second. "Goodbye." She went to the truck.

To see a fine lady upon a white horse —

Andy couldn't stand the pain. Big baby or not she was willing to do anything to stop it. "Regina!" she cried, running after her. She heard Clover whine behind her, straining at her leash. "Regina!" She leapt onto the diamond tread of the running board on the passenger side and pulled at the shiny T-handle. "Regina!" she shouted through the window as she heard the brakes release.

Regina put the brakes on again and slid to unlock the door.

Andy scrambled in.

"You can't leave again. I can't take it if you leave again."

"You don't act like you want to see me."

"I want to see you. It just hurts. I thought I'd die when you left. Please, Regina!"

"Please what, Andy? I don't know what you want."

She rocked on the seat. This isn't how I want to be, she thought. Not Regina, not anyone would want her like this. *How am I supposed to stand it? First I have the Studebaker back, now Regina?* The huge motor purred in front of them. "Just go. Just drive. Show me your truck."

Willing Jas, Clover, Gramma, the Studebaker, and her friends from her consciousness, as if the past months had never happened, Andy watched Regina work the transmission stick. Her mind was a jumble of nursery rhymes again. *Humpty Dumpty sat on a wall,/Humpty Dumpty had a great fall;/All the kings horses/And all the king's men/Couldn't put Humpty Dumpty together again.*

What did all the king's men know about her anyway? She was the only one who could put herself back together again. This was real life. Nonsense rhymes would do her no good.

Nonsense rhymes? Wasn't that another name for them? Had Gramma filled her head with nothing but nonsense? Had she spent her whole life listening to the shrieks of raving clowns in her head?

Regina pulled at the steering wheel as if it were salt water taffy, tugging and tugging until they were around a corner. "I practiced on the hills back home. I knew I'd get back out here. But I'll tell you, a couple of hills is one thing; San Francisco is not exactly a road runner's paradise."

They could have been anywhere — Ohio, New Hampshire. There was nothing in the world but her own pain and Regina. From the corner of her eye Andy recognized the Castro, then Divisadero Street.

"You don't know how gutsy it feels to be up here trundling through San Francisco."

Andy didn't feel gutsy, she felt like a wrung-out wash rag.

Regina took 101 toward the Presidio. The Golden Gate Bridge lay out there, full of promise, the crown of Banbury Cross.

"How I've dreamed of driving over that sucker," Regina said, an exultant look on her face.

"I've never done it." Had she been waiting to share this with Regina? How much else had she held back from Jas?

"And now we are, shaggy, craggy Andy! Everything's just the way I wanted it to be!"

"You really wanted to do this with me?"

"I wanted to be with you again, but I didn't want to be some scared woman hanging on your coattails. I wanted to be able to make it on my own. You pulled me out of Weirs Beach the first time, but this time I drove myself out of there in this baby."

Andy hadn't realized it before, but it had been her car, her race, her impetus that had empowered them both. She hadn't been a big baby back then, hadn't felt sorry for herself one minute.

Now Regina wanted to show off her own power. It made her feel good to know Regina had come back to do that, but was that all Regina wanted? Did it matter who she showed off to? Had she already shown off to Roy? To Verne? To Jenny Alder? Or was Regina just showing off for Regina?

Andy chastised herself. She should be glad for Regina's good fortune, not mean about it. And after all, here they were doing what she'd wanted also. Even if the truck wasn't that old Studebaker, Regina sat beside her. She should try to enjoy this rough ride, the thousand gear shifts, the smell of warm vinyl and dust and discarded orange peels that filled the cab.

"Where are we going?"

"I don't know. I dropped my last load. The broker won't have anything for me until tomorrow or the day after. I've got some bucks. How about a fun run to Oregon? Seattle? Alaska?" Regina's smile was full of mischief and adventure.

"Just like that? What about —" she almost said Jas "— about that old Studebaker?"

"Park it for a while. We've got other wheels now. Isn't this how we always were? Crazy and free?"

"We? Is there a we?"

"I thought there was. I didn't know you'd be this upset, handsome, especially after all this time. I really liked riding with you, Andy, settling in new towns together for a while." There was the hurt look again, as if Andy had somehow been the one to tear up Regina's heart, not the other way around. "I can't be lovers with you anymore, but I do want to be friends."

Regina's words were like a slab of concrete fallen on Andy's heart.

"I need freedom, Andy, that's why trucking is for me. I can live anywhere. There's a whole new experience any place I go. I'm having a love affair with the road, with the whole U.S. of A. And that's just what I need right now. I want to tell you the whole story."

"You need freedom, but you want to be with me. I don't understand."

"Neither do I, but I know I don't want to lose you again. You're my best friend. I've missed you a lot."

The traffic was thick. They were almost on the bridge. Regina pulled impatiently on the leather thong that sounded the air horn. "Every time I pull that horn I get cold chills!"

Something in Andy said to jump out of the truck now, before they went over the bridge together, before it was too late.

Instead, that brave anger she'd swallowed too long sprang from her mouth. Nonsense rhymes hadn't been as scary. "What am I supposed to do while you're off being free? Hole up in a room in some queer-hating town while you're down the street with your freedom? Or would you go out on the road to fool around? Then come back for me? Pack up, Andy, we're going to Missoula!"

In her head Andy could hear Starr, Kyle, Tolliver, Windy, Jas and Nicholas cheering her anger. Gramma was saying, *Stick up for yourself!* "I just don't get it. What do you want?"

"A companion, some kind of family off and sometimes on the road. I want you in my life, Sweet Andy, but I can't do it the way we did before." Regina smiled as if sharing a delicious secret with her. "Maybe we'll both have girls in every port."

She stared at Regina, so high above the road, in horror. The woman was just plain selfish, as if what she wanted was the only thing that counted. As if the life they'd made together had meant nothing. Jasmine Jones would never do this, would she?

Yet, when Regina turned to look at her again, behind those eyes was the soft needing woman that called to Andy. It was that woman who wanted somebody to come home to, someplace to call her own, a friend. It was that woman who loved Andy and who she, Andy, still loved back. If she spent some time with Regina, that woman would return, would shed the hard defiant short-haired truck driver queen-of-the-road who'd almost taken her over.

But that wouldn't be half as exciting as the whole Regina, bad as well as good.

Was that true? Wasn't Jas exciting, and exciting in a way that didn't hurt her? *Mary, Mary quite contrary,/How does your garden grow?/With silver bells, and cockleshells/And pretty maids all in a row.*

Could Regina, could any one person have it both ways all at the same time? Maybe that was okay, Andy thought. Maybe I'm the one being selfish to want all of Regina's love. Maybe I could live like this for a while, a year, even get used to it. I know how to make friends now, and Regina would come home for good some time. Just because Ma and Dad did it one way, was that the only way? It was what she and Regina had between them that mattered, not how they worked it out.

Why was Regina's way of thinking starting to make sense even though a few minutes ago it sounded crazy?

All of a sudden Andy's life in San Francisco seemed so small. It had only been a little while with Jas, and then she hadn't made a move until Jas had felt as exciting as Regina. What were two-week vacations compared to the grand adventure Regina offered? What was her Chattanooga Street garage worth compared to working on this truck, getting a bunch of different jobs all over?

"Do you like dogs?"

"You know my family always had one," Regina answered with a smile. "I was the one who dragged them home."

What did she really have but a rented room, a dog and a car?

The Bay glittered beneath them. The world felt wider than it ever had before up here on this span of metal, in a great dragon of a truck, Regina beside her.

CHAPTER TWENTY-ONE

When the Alexander exit to Sausalito came into sight the magnet of the road lost its pull. Andy could catch a ferry in Sausalito and maybe be back in time to have lunch with Jas.

Jas! How would she feel if she called the shop at lunchtime and Nicholas told her? She couldn't just take off on that sweet, honest woman. But this was Regina beside her.

"Can we stop in Sausalito?"

"I was hoping to get to the coast by afternoon."

"No, Regina. I'm not ready to go." Once again she was astonished at herself.

"You got it." The empty truck clanged down the ramp and onto the descending, abruptly curving road. Regina found her way to the end of town, where she parked next to an abandoned railway and raised her sunglasses to the top of her head.

"Want to go exploring?" asked Regina, one of her gentle touches on Andy's arm.

Andy wanted to sit right there and make up her mind. She wanted to call Starr and ask him what to do now. She wanted Windy to tell her an old story just like hers and Regina's so she'd have an example to follow. She wished Tolliver were there to blast her with the truth and tell Regina off.

It was exhausting, not knowing what to do. She walked with Regina past weathered buildings and ship hulls onto Bridgeway, the main street in Sausalito. Houseboats bobbed on the bay.

"Don't look so miserable, Sweet Andy, or I'm just going to go on without you," said Regina, walking quickly, her black leather jacket, tough yet devastatingly feminine, flapping open in the stiff, sunny-warm ocean wind.

Regina the truck driver, Andy thought, trying to get used to the idea. With rings on her fingers and bells on her toes.

"What happened back home, Regina? Did they bug you about being gay?"

Regina laughed. "You think I'd care if they did? My world's gotten a whole lot bigger than it was that summer when I still cared what Weirs Beach thought." She patted Andy's hand. "Your family doesn't know and neither does mine. I had to stare down a lot of the kids, but I think some of them kind of admire what we did. Especially you taking on Roy and winning against all his noisy power. He joined the Army not two weeks after we left. My old girlfriends feel trapped, changing Pampers, never getting to see the world. They wanted to hear about all the places I'd been. It'd be okay to go back if you wanted to suffocate."

"I don't know," Andy said. "At least you look normal."

Regina slipped her arm through Andy's, just like she used to. Being honest wasn't scaring Regina away.

Her arm felt bruised where Regina held it. *She doesn't want to be my lover,* she repeated to herself. *But this is how she acted when she did.* It felt all wrong. She dropped the arm as if it were hot and melting too.

In her mouth, her throat, her lungs, the salty air felt like balm. Andy realized that it was some part of her brain that had melted in there, under the heat of Regina's touch. She couldn't get one thought unstuck from another.

Wouldn't Windy laugh, Andy thought, to see me running off with Regina, the wrong woman.

She pictured Tolliver playing music in the desert because love Ruby as she might, Tolliver couldn't be with her.

What if Jas was crying on Nicholas's shoulder, then taking Clover home with her, storing the Studebaker, moving Andy's things to her apartment, lovingly folding them into boxes? Hoping.

She remembered Starr and Kyle looking into each

other's eyes. The look haunted her. It held years in it, years she wanted.

"I'm not going to push you into anything." Regina touched her hand. "I've been to hell and back this year, getting loose and then putting myself together again. I longed for your comfort. You always felt so safe to me, Andy."

"This is feeling like a goodbye. Don't do it, Regina."

"I have no right to your comfort and safety, Andy. It's borrowed, maybe even stolen. I have to get some of my own. You don't even want what I can give anymore, do you?"

"Regina —" Andy was glad that she'd forgotten the camera. She might have been tempted to settle for a bunch of paper memories.

Regina grasped Andy's arm, caressing it. "You're the one who's left me this time, Sweet Andy. You wouldn't hurt a spider on the wall, how can I expect you to say anything you're afraid will hurt me? You don't want me anymore."

"I don't want you anymore?"

Andy felt like she was standing on a little strip of land. Was Sausalito rooted to the ocean floor or did it just float there, like all the houseboats, waiting for an earthquake to sever it? She shook.

"Come on. I'll walk you to the ferry."

Andy felt like she was walking on a wooden slip out over Lake Winnepesaukee, rocking on the waves beneath her.

"Talk to me, Andy. I don't know when I'll see you again."

She turned to Regina and pulled her tight against her. Into her hair she said, "I have a girl.

227

Her name's Jasmine Jones. And a dog named Clover. I'm fixing cars for money."

"Everything you've always wanted."

"Except you."

Regina's arms tightened around her. "Who am I? I sure don't know."

"Regina, you need to stay! I can take care of you!"

"Hell, Andy. It must be a bitch just taking care of yourself. Don't go taking care of somebody else. Me or Jasmine Jones."

"She doesn't need me."

"But she wants you."

The implication was another blow. Andy drew back, just looking at Regina. "Why? Why don't you?"

"I have to want me first or I don't have a thing to give you or anyone else."

They walked again, not touching, to the foot of Anchor Street. The ferry was waiting.

"I have to walk across that gangplank away from you?"

They were both crying.

"I'm not going to ask you anymore to come with me. You know it's not right."

"But we're married, Regina. I mean inside. I feel married to you."

"Don't hold on so tight."

They looked at each other. The attendant was untying the ropes. She backed away from Regina. Andy wouldn't turn away from her. She stumbled at the connection to the ferry, but righted herself.

Regina pulled a handkerchief from a pocket and wiped her eyes, blew her nose. With a sad smile on her face, Regina didn't move forward, didn't walk away, just stood there. What had Feather said about a special demon? Poor Regina, Andy thought, had no one waiting for her anywhere. No Jas, no Nicholas, no Clover.

"No," she said, stepping clear of the gangplank. "I can't go back to them, Regina. Not with this longing for you. It's not fair."

"Okay. If that's what you want."

They walked south on Bridgeway. It was still early and the tourists were just beginning to filter into town. They found a phone. She remembered the last time she'd gone looking for one, when Regina had already been on her way to San Francisco.

"It's me," she said to Nicholas. "I won't be back in today."

Regina unwrapped a piece of gum a few feet away. Her profile was as striking as Andy had remembered it, and even more appealing under the white coastal sunshine. In a low voice Andy asked Nicholas, "Could you keep Clover a while?"

He asked what was going on and she told him.

"Tell Jas I'm just friends with Regina now, okay?" When Nicholas laughed, she protested, "It's true."

Even as she said it, looking at Regina, her heart filled with a hope she knew she shouldn't have — the friendship was only true for Regina.

They made their way back to the truck and headed north on the interstate through Petaluma, Santa Rosa, Ukiah. The little grape-growing towns fell behind them like the months without Regina. It was a luxury, being with Regina, her voice filling the cab with talk, with laughter.

"Uncle Jack let me hitch rides with the other

drivers till I got used to the big trucks. Then I was running two-man for a while, spelling whoever needed me. They'd stay awake long enough to teach me their trucks, and turn me loose."

"With all those men?"

"Uncle Jack told them hands off or he'd have their jobs. I never had so much protection in my life as I do on the road. Everyplace I go I know somebody who knows somebody. I can take care of myself, but it doesn't hurt to have these guys watching out for me. And the women too, the wives that ride."

She told her about Jody.

"What's she drive?"

"I didn't notice. I have a picture back at my room."

"Didn't notice! You will. After this trip you'll know them all. This is an International Transtar, needs some paint and it doesn't have a lot of pretty chrome, but it holds its own with those big old Kenworths and Petes. Even passes them sometimes. I pull a Great Dane trailer. Maybe I should have left it back there, but I'll want it when I call my broker." She flashed a grin at Andy. "I wouldn't mind mixing a little business with pleasure. Talk to me, Sweet Andy. Tell me about your year."

She did then, remembering the Holiday Inn cornfield, Willa and her family, the minister, Starr and Kyle, meeting Tolliver, then going to Tucson. As she talked she was aware of the need to be touching Regina, of an urge so deep she might have been born with it, to dance with her.

"You chased the thieves?" cried Regina when she got to the theft of the Studebaker.

"Windy did, and Tolliver boomed away at them with the shotgun. I was in the back seat praying."

Regina took her hand off the wheel and squeezed Andy's arm briefly. "Then what?"

By the time she finished the part about stealing the Studebaker back, Regina was grinning widely. "That's the Andy I like to remember. The daredevil, not the one who sat out on the porch in Columbus, too tired to go anywhere."

Regina took her eyes off the road to meet hers for so long Andy grew nervous and looked away. Or maybe it was the look in those eyes. They glittered and measured. Something passed between them, something familiar yet scary. Andy's stomach churned from it. Unobtrusively, she shifted the sopping seam of her overalls away from her crotch.

"I want to call Jas tonight."

"Sure thing, babycakes."

Regina let out a cry of such exultant freedom when she reached the wild Pacific for the first time that there was no staying away from her. She grabbed Andy's hand and they ran along the water line, ran through the roaring sound of ocean until they staggered. Then, laughing, they began to walk back.

"Look!" Andy said again, picking up a weathered oyster shell. "Silver bells and cockleshells!"

Regina raised her manicured eyebrows. "Whatever you say, little Andy."

The sunset was only a rosy line on the horizon. Andy felt like a kid. Was that good? It had felt better when she and Jas ate ice cream before dinner — that was just playing at being kids. Now she felt as helpless as she had on the lake shore the day of Gramma's funeral. She'd fled from the adults and stood in her short dress, patent leather shoes and white anklets facing the whipping winter wind, her tears close to freezing on her cheeks. She'd barely been able to breathe, the wind had been so strong, and she'd felt it howling right through her tiny chest. It had been sunset then, too, but the sky had been nearly as gray as the white-capped lake.

At last Regina had come back. "I can't believe I'm here with you," Andy said.

Regina still clung to her hand. "It's awesome, isn't it?"

They found a Chinese restaurant in an old house and stuffed themselves at dinner. She noticed the phone booth outside the Thunderbird, but bypassed it. Later, she thought, unwilling to give up a moment of the feeling of her hand in Regina's.

The right time to call came while she lay on the bed listening to the sound of Regina's running bath. Had it been providence that had filled the motel in April so there had been only one room left, with one bed in it? What would happen tonight?

She switched on the TV to soothe the churning which, she now realized, was not in her stomach, but lower, about where her pubic hair began. Images of the old *Mission Impossible* pushed away images of Jas. She'd waited a long time to be where she was right now. The rest was tomorrow. Or was it yesterday?

The bath water was draining. The churning

turned into a flutter. She watched a character on TV try to steal a virus from a sealed chamber. Could she do it before the enemy scientists walked in? She knew exactly the character's feeling of fear. She was alone in her adventure too. Only her own virus was fear.

Certainly it had been providential for Jody the truck driver to come by when she had. Jody who'd shut herself up tight after her lover died just like Andy had after Gramma had gone and after her parents had turned their backs on her to start having other kids. She knew how it felt to be all alone in the world at the age of seven. It felt like getting sick. That's when she'd gotten sick the first time. Until now, she'd forgotten all about having pneumonia after Gramma died.

The bathroom door opened. Andy wouldn't look. Her clitoris was screaming for attention. She should have touched herself while Regina bathed. It would have made the night easier. Could she sleep in the truck? No, a night with Regina, even without a wink of sleep, was worth it. Regina had saved her from being Jody, only she didn't know how to be the saved Andy without Regina at her side to keep her well.

She heard Regina cross the room just as the TV star shut the virus into a safe carrying case and slipped it into the pocket of her smock.

Regina sat on the edge of the bed. She smelled approximately the way heaven would. She was rubbing something into her calves. Was that her bare shoulder reflected on the TV screen?

Regina's hand and arm came across her. She

233

looked good in that short hair, younger and more innocent. Her closeness made Andy light-headed. She lay her head against Andy's chest.

"I need to talk to you."

Andy took a deep breath and put one arm around Regina.

"After I left Columbus I started to have nightmares," Regina said against her chest. "I dreamed that something big was crushing me and I was helpless. I couldn't be alone and Verne wasn't interested. I persuaded her to take me along when she went to Chicago. The nightmares got better for a while, but Verne was doing a lot of drugs and there I was, let loose in a city with thousands of available women."

Regina shifted to lie next to her, snuggled under her arm. "What can I say, Andy? I went wild. I needed to sow some oats, I thought, but the nightmares got worse the more women I saw."

Her words hurt, thought Andy, but might lead somewhere, to some explanation that would feel better.

"I slept with white women, Indian women, a Chinese woman, two African women from the art school who were lovers. Butch women and femme women, heavy ones, old ones, baby dykes. College women and women just out of prison and just out of marriages. I was insatiable. I couldn't spend a night alone. I did women like Verne did drugs. I knew I should be careful about AIDS, but I just couldn't stop. And with almost every one of them sex was wild, great, beautiful. But when I woke up the next morning I couldn't stand to be with them. I hated them. I pushed them away when they came on to me. I was rude. I was cruel. I ran. I never saw one of them a second time."

Regina shifted closer. "What was wrong with me? I left Chicago with a woman, but after one night I couldn't be in her car. I was still living on some money Verne had given me — her family is rich — and I took a bus to Tucson where somebody knew somebody. I swore there'd be no more sex. I'd get a job and take long walks in the desert to bake this craziness out of me. In Tucson I started out sleeping in a tent on the women's land where you looked for me. I was free of nightmares there. The nights were full of new sounds and smells. I slept in a sleeping bag right on the ground. If I hadn't been afraid of snakes and scorpions and spiders I wouldn't have used the tent at all. Even though I didn't have the dreams, when I woke in the mornings I was terrified for the first few minutes, as if someone frightening had just left. I started waking before dawn with this sense and this fear. I'd be soaking wet with sweat, and between my legs too, as if I was excited. But I wasn't making love with anybody, Andy. It was just me and the desert."

Andy didn't say a word. So Regina had been in trouble, she thought. She'd been hurting in her own way.

"The fear came earlier and earlier. After about a week I couldn't sleep at all. Feather noticed me looking haggard and we started talking. She told me that it sounded like I was trying to remember something, something that had gotten under my skin so bad it was making me crazy. But what? I walked the desert trails with a canteen over my shoulder and a big hat shading me, torturing it out of my memory. I had no idea what was festering in there. One night Feather had some women over. Her — I can't say it to this day."

Regina fell silent for so long Andy thought she might be sleeping. Then she felt Regina's tears fall on her arm, warm and chilling all at once.

"Her *incest* survivors' group," Regina said with the sound of clenched teeth. "There were nine women there who met once a month to tell what had happened if they needed to, or to let new women tell their stories. I felt so scared and sick that I got up to leave. But the women coaxed me back. They held me and fed me chamomile tea. I didn't want to, but I started crying and crying. I still didn't know why. They wrapped me in a blanket and I told them about the nightmares, the fear in the mornings. One woman talked about how her father had lain on top of her and she'd thought she would suffocate, just a little girl, not able to breathe, but when she cried, he put a hand over her mouth and that's when it got crystal clear for me. I smelled Jacques, Uncle Jack."

"Your uncle? The one with the trucks?"

"Yes. His aftershave came back to me. And I felt his bristly cheek against mine. But he used his huge squishy lips to shut me up. As the woman described what else her father had done I knew that what Jacques had done to me had been wrong. It may sound strange to you, but I'd always just accepted what he did. I'd known it had happened all along, but I hadn't put it together with that crushed feeling or the nightmares. I didn't know I could be furious about it. Over the next weeks when I woke up with the fear I made myself picture him. I made my body remember him. I listened to the women when they told me he'd damaged me. I got mad."

She sat upright, away from Andy's hold. "The women were all trying to remember what was buried in them at these meetings. I was the only one who hadn't buried it. But I was no different from them. It had still driven me nuts. They talked about what it was like for them now. One couldn't let anyone touch her, female or male. Another spent just over three years with every lover before she lost interest. She thought that was probably how long the incest had gone on. A woman who had been married fourteen years remembered her childhood one night during sex and tried to kill her husband. I wasn't the only one who'd tried to use sex to cover up the memory. There was a seventeen-year-old in the group who figured she'd been with over three hundred women and men. She'd also tried to kill herself twice. Most of them were drunks or druggies. I was lucky. I was just easy."

"No."

"Yes, Andy. I was." Regina leaned on one elbow, facing her. "Before you I felt nothing. I did it with every man who interested me at all and I was cold as ice. I woke up with you. And that's what the women said happened. You woke me up. Once I started feeling safe, all the feelings I'd buried started leaking back out. I loved Uncle Jack, I hated him. I'd never been able to feel all that because none of it was what I really felt: anger and terror. I'd always used sex to keep those feelings back so I cheated on you, looking to forget again."

"You mean I can't have you because of what Uncle Jack did way back then?"

The room felt cold. Andy got up to turn the thermostat higher. If only she'd known Regina was so scared, felt as alone as she did. But when they'd gotten together neither of them had thought a thing about having winds howling inside them. That's just the way things were. You could adjust a thermostat, but not your insides.

Regina wrapped her robe more tightly around herself and offered the extra blanket to her. Andy sat cross-legged, facing Regina, and huddled in the blanket. The water surged outside.

"It wasn't anything I did," Andy said.

"No. It had nothing to do with you at all. Except that you were so safe I began to heal with you, Andy. I'll always love you for that. Do you want to hear more?"

"All of it. I want to understand."

"I don't know if I understand. I feel like I just blundered along trying whatever might work. There was a woman in Tucson, Jenny Alder, who'd been after me since I got there. I wanted to see if, now that I remembered, I could be with someone. That was a holy mess. She was the roughest woman lover I'd ever had, and then would get mad when I couldn't come. I think she was drawn to my craziness."

Regina hugged herself. Her chest rose and fell rapidly. She sighed as if to get enough air to go on. "I had to move on. I didn't know what I was looking for, or who, or how I'd get it, but I wanted to keep heading west. And all this time I was considering doing what some of the women in the group had done to lay their demons to rest — go home and confront the devil. I guess I just had to run farther before I could turn around and retrace my steps."

"That's when you came out here?"

Regina nodded. "It was too beautiful to spoil. All the places I'd traveled felt dirty; I didn't want to ruin San Francisco or any new place ever again so I got a ride back as far as Kansas City and took the bus home from there with my last money. I thought of hitching, but I was afraid I'd kill any man who started up with me. All those days on the road I thought about how much I liked to travel. I still had this restlessness inside me, and it was about Pittsburgh when I put together that I needed to confront Uncle Jack."

"Weren't you scared of him?"

"I can't tell you how much. But what more could he do to me? I marched into his house. My ears were roaring like all my anger and all my fear were screaming to get out. They almost paralyzed me. Some women talked with their mothers first, but I knew my business was with Jack and only Jack. He and his country-clubbing wife had a living room full of company. Well, I dragged him into another room and yelled, so I could hear myself over my roaring ears, that I wasn't going to keep quiet any more."

Andy cheered. "All right, Regina!"

"He surprised me. He didn't try to shut me up. I think he's sorry, but he wouldn't come right out and say it. He asked what he could do to make up for it, said he'd felt lousy about it for years, then asked if I'd like to learn trucking. That suited my restlessness and I took him up on it. But I told him I wasn't sitting on my secret no matter what he did."

Regina's eyes looked tired, and tender. "So here I am, Andy. The roaring comes back now and then. I know I'm still scarred. I may not ever get all the way well. I don't want to be with you and hurt you again. I don't even know if I can be with anyone again. I don't know if I can make love or come without crying, or stay with a woman no matter how much I love her."

They were holding hands. Regina went on. "I headed straight for you because, like I said, you feel so safe. But I see what it's doing to you, wanting me, and how afraid you are of me. I didn't mean to cut you down. You were the only safe person in my life. Your girl in San Francisco is probably wonderful to you and will stick around. You're lucky you can do it. Maybe I can, too, someday. But not now, even if what I thought was dead inside me about you isn't after all."

Andy reached to stroke Regina's face. Why couldn't they have learned all this together, in each other's arms? But it hadn't happened that way, and there was nothing she could do about it, just like there wasn't a thing she could have done about Gramma or her folks. At least Regina wasn't Gramma. Her legacy wouldn't be nonsense rhymes, but rules for living life.

"You may have gotten out of Weirs Beach in my car, Regina, but so did I," Andy said. "I thought you were saving me, not you."

"Really?"

Andy nodded. "That's why it felt so bad when

you left. I wasn't saved at all. I was still Andy Blaine, only now I wasn't even home. I felt like I was a little kid again, all alone, but I wasn't. I'm not. If I went off with you tomorrow into the wild blue yonder I'd still be hanging onto your coattails. In San Francisco everybody thinks I'm grown up. I have to take care of myself here. I can't afford to act like I'm seven and the world just ended. I don't want to give up. I've come this far, I want to go for it."

"For what?"

Andy searched through all the nursery rhymes jammed into her head, but couldn't come up with an answer. So she laughed and said, "Darned if I know."

"You *have* changed, Andy. Once you'd have hung your head, looked ashamed, and spent days trying to figure out how to answer. I like it when you say no to me, and I like your laugh even better."

"Someday maybe I'll know, if anyone can know what they're really going after. I do know I'm glad I came out, and I wouldn't have without you."

"Bullcrap. You're too good-looking to stay straight. There are dykes in Weirs Beach. I saw two in the arcades when I was there."

"Off season? Another Regina and Andy?" They laughed and hugged. "I want Jas. But that's all I know about what I want."

Regina looked up at her. There was a warmth and a sparkle in her eyes as well as tiredness. "Maybe that's what keeps us going then, Andy, the mystery." Regina's tears weren't over. "It's so goddamned sad. I love you, Andy Blaine."

Andy let herself go then too. "Yeah," she rasped

into Regina's hair. "I can't stand it." Regina held her tighter.

They cried together, alternately holding and offering each other tissues. After a while she thought about white light, and green healing light, and blanketed them in both until they fell asleep.

CHAPTER TWENTY-TWO

Jas looked blankly at her, a hurt anger in her red-rimmed eyes. "You came back," she said.

"I'm sorry I went off like that. I love you, Jas."

Jasmine's words were tight, low, accusatory. "That was a pretty cruddy way to treat someone you love."

"I didn't know what to do."

"Obviously you did, Andy. You ran off with *her.*"

"Not for, not for," she started, but didn't want to lie. "It wasn't finished. We were married."

"Tell me you went to Vegas and got a divorce. Together."

"I feel divorced now. A friendly divorce."

Jas yanked on the spigot at her sink and dragged the hose onto the porch. Andy stood in the doorway, not knowing what else to say.

Jas watered the planters and started on the potato cans.

"I didn't do anything with her. She told me what's wrong. It's because her un—"

For the first time Jas raised her voice with Andy. "I do not want to know!"

"But —"

"No! Read my lips: N.O." Jas plugged her ears with her fingers.

"Okay," she shouted. "Okay!"

They looked at each other in the late afternoon light. She couldn't see any fog behind Jasmine, over the yard, but she smelled it, tasted it, knew it hung invisible in the air waiting to gather and soften the city, the harsh words of lovers.

"I understand that you had to see her, to work it out, but why didn't you call me? I was afraid you'd left forever."

"No way, Jas."

"You didn't know that."

"I know now."

Tearless, but fearful, Jas had looked in her eyes then. Andy thought, *Love's a risky thing for everybody.*

She'd moved in with Jas not long after that and they'd been preparing for today, for the parade, ever since. While Jas showered, Andy dressed, looking at the wall of photographs she'd created on her side of the bed: the portrait of Starr and Kyle in their old-fashioned clothes; desert dawns and flowers; Tolliver flexing her muscles as she held up tumbleweed. There were the abandoned buildings of Shamrock, Texas and the kerchiefed old woman with the accent, the dog walker from Starr and Kyle's Chicago stoop, Willa's family at the fairground. Several showed Clover chasing sticks in San Francisco parks. And then there was long-haired Windy dwarfed by a cactus, that clown at the Civic Center, Jas and Clover by the Airflyte and Nicholas, gold teeth shining, in front of a Packard — and the poodles Miss Kitty and Dorothy Lamour.

Framed, there was the enlargement she'd made of Regina and that old Studebaker under a palm tree on Dolores Street. They'd driven directly back to the garage. Then Regina had primped and stood stiffly posed in her skin-tight pants like a fifties movie star — one arm outstretched, chin lifted. Her smile looked forced and she'd worn sunglasses to cover her tear-puffed eyes.

Below it was the snapshot Andy had stolen. She and Regina had walked back to the truck and Regina had hugged her goodbye, then climbed up to the cab. She'd been smiling, but her chin quivered. Then she'd swung out from the top step, hanging onto the door handle, one arm and one leg outstretched, crying, "What a gorgeous city! I'm so glad I'll have someone to visit!" and Andy had caught her.

The picture was crooked, but very, very clear. It was the exuberant, troubled Regina she loved.

Nicholas had laughed at her when she'd described the image of Regina rattling around the country. "That's sheer conceit!" he'd said.

"I'm not conceited."

"You're blowing up your importance in the world if you think Regina can't get along just fine without you, if you think you can predict her fate. I'm sure she misses you, but life does go on, babe. Remember I've seen this ghost from your past in person, talked to her. I know how brash and competent and lovely she looked. How totally capable she sounded of taking care of herself — and of chewing you up and spitting you out."

So here Andy was, in the middle of life going on, just as if the vision of Regina hadn't dropped out of the air and whisked her off to the coast two months ago.

Jas had come back in the room pinkly clean, buffing her hair into its usual feathery look. Seeing Jas, it occurred to Andy that Regina had only been a stop for *her*, too, on the way to fun, laughing Jas. Kind, forgiving Jas.

At exactly 6:30 a.m. that old Studebaker, polished to a sparkle, stopped at the inn. Nicholas pulled up a few minutes later and lugged lavender crepe paper, glue, staplers, a feather boa, red, white and blue top hats, and a huge gay flag from his truck.

"Great day for a parade!" he said. They decorated the car and themselves for the next two hours.

"The final touch," announced Jas. She bent in her top hat and tied a lavender ribbon onto Clover's collar. Immediately Clover rolled onto her back, presenting her stomach for a scratch.

"Clover, you horse's ass, don't get your uniform dirty."

Andy couldn't stand the happiness she felt, seeing Jas and Clover next to each other, like a family, smiling at her. She was wearing out the pomegranate seeds in her pocket, fingering them with nervous excitement.

Nicholas looked at his watch. "Uh-oh," he said, "the stars are late." He wore red coveralls with a gay flag patch sewed onto one breast pocket and a small American flag sewed across his bottom. "Maybe they passed laws about burning the thing, but nobody said I can't put nationalism and capitalism in their place. Yet."

The door of the informally christened Lesbian Inn flew open and Umeko, in shocking pink short shorts and a baggy blouse, came down the steps, her tall boots fringed lavender. She accepted her top hat with her usual cool dignity.

Cricket came next, in oversized shorts and a new white sweatshirt with large lavender letters that read simply PRIDE. She darted here and there surveying and approving their work.

Behind them Meg came through the door, turned around and went back in, emerged with a book bag, came to the bottom of the steps and ran back up. "I forgot to pee!" she called.

Cricket and Umeko unrolled the banners. THE LESBIAN INN, proclaimed one. The others brought tears to Andy's eyes: MUSKETEER AUTOWORKS.

Nicholas and Andy trundled the flat five-foot trailer out of the garage and attached it to the hitch they'd welded on the back of the Studebaker. Jas,

Umeko and Cricket stretched the banners from the top of their posts to the edge of the trailer. When Meg returned, more flustered than ever, she was installed on a throne bolted to the trailer bed. Umeko put the gay flag in Meg's hand and Nicholas wrapped the pink feather boa around her.

Meg and Nicholas squeezed inside the car with them for the ride downtown. Clover tried to lick Meg's sequins off.

"There they are," Andy said in a hushed whisper as they began to snake through the crowded side streets. To think she'd never liked cities. "Are they really all gay?"

Everyone laughed.

"They might be ten percent straight," Umeko said. "But it's unlikely. I mean, why in the world would God make so many straights? You know She considers them an abomination."

A marshall directed them into the lineup.

"Nice car!" called a woman from the Dykes On Bikes contingent.

"Nice bike!" answered Nicholas as he and Meg took their places on the float.

Andy wiped her palms on her coveralls for the hundredth time.

"Nervous?" asked Jas.

"Yes. A little."

Slowly, like a great rousing beast, each segment of the parade began to move. When her turn came Andy stepped on the gas too hard, then braked to compensate. Meg shrieked behind them. Cricket leaned out the back window. "You okay?"

"What's a little whiplash for a good cause?" Nicholas called.

Andy drove smoothly after that, though that meant missing most of the people on the sidelines. Some were as costumed as the marchers. The Sisters of Perpetual Indulgence seemed to be everywhere, blessing the crowds. Andy laughed every time she spotted one. And then she saw her.

"Tolliver!" she screamed out her window. "Tolliver! Tolliver!"

"Andy!" Tolliver loped over to the car, bent under her backpack, a saxophone case swinging from each hand. "You got her back!"

Mandy Tolliver's smile was as big as ever and made Andy laugh just as it always had. "Yeah! They didn't hurt her a bit," answered Andy.

Tolliver was jogging beside the car, peering in.

"Hi, Regina," said Tolliver.

She almost slammed on the brakes, but remembered Meg and Nicholas just in time. "No, Tolliver. The *Studebaker*. I got my car back. *This* is Jasmine Jones."

"Hi, Tolliver," said Jas, with her sunny smile. "Natural mistake."

"Big bozo mistake! I'm sorry, Jasmine. I just got to town. Windy claimed she needed a rest."

Tolliver climbed onto the float and played Dixieland for the rest of the parade.

The thicker the crowd got, the louder the cheers. Between the Dixieland and the applause Andy soon found tears dripping from her eyes.

"Are you all right?" asked Jas, rubbing the arm that had been waving out the window for half an hour.

"I'm just happy."

"Why, Andy Blaine, I don't think I've ever heard

you admit that before." Jas reached across Clover to take her hand.

"I don't know if I ever felt it before. Home again, home again, jiggety jig."

"It does feel like home, doesn't it?"

The crowds applauded, the sun shone strong. Andy was moving through a city of people like herself. What more could she want?

"You know what I hope?"

"What?" asked Jas.

"I hope Regina can find this too someday. This happy lasting feeling." She tried to imagine it, but knew it was a long way off. At least she'd admitted that she couldn't give happiness to Regina. She was just shifting into second, feeling that gratified feeling she got about the gears chonking exactly into place when she realized that she probably couldn't have made Willa happy either.

"I don't want to hear about Regina, Andy, okay?" said Jasmine, passing her a handkerchief. "It's our day."

"Okay, I'm sorry." She blew her nose. "I never used to cry," Andy told her, "when I was unhappy. How come I cry when I'm happy?"

Cricket suggested, "Because you're gay?"

"And am I!" Andy said. "Queerer than a three-dollar bill!"

"As a bull-dagger!" cried Cricket.

"As a limp-wristed drag queen!" Umeko shouted out the window at Dorothy from Oz on roller skates.

"Hi, Sister!" he called. Clover barked at him, tail wagging.

Someone yelled from the sidelines. "Look at that

old Studebaker! Did you really bring her all the way from New Hampshire?"

"You bet!" she shouted back.

She *had* brought the Studebaker, it hadn't brought her. She'd traveled across America, steered through life in her Studebaker, to get someplace where it was safe to say, "I'm happy."

THAT OLD STUDEBAKER by Lee Lynch. 272 pp. Andy's affair
with Regina and her attachment to her beloved car.
ISBN 0-941483-82-7 $9.95

PASSION'S LEGACY by Lori Paige. 224 pp. Sarah is swept into
the arms of Augusta Pym in this delightful historical romance.
ISBN 0-941483-81-9   8.95

THE PROVIDENCE FILE by Amanda Kyle Williams. 256 pp.
Second espionage thriller featuring lesbian agent Madison McGuire
ISBN 0-941483-92-4   8.95

I LEFT MY HEART by Jaye Maiman. 320 pp. A Robin Miller
Mystery. First in a series.   ISBN 0-941483-72-X   9.95

THE PRICE OF SALT by Patricia Highsmith (writing as Claire
Morgan). 288 pp. Classic lesbian novel, first issued in 1952 . . .
acknowledged by its author under her own, very famous, name.
ISBN 1-56280-003-5   8.95

SIDE BY SIDE by Isabel Miller. 256 pp. From beloved author of
Patience and Sarah.   ISBN 0-941483-77-0   8.95

SOUTHBOUND by Sheila Ortiz Taylor. 240 pp. Hilarious sequel
to *Faultline.*   ISBN 0-941483-78-9   8.95

STAYING POWER: LONG TERM LESBIAN COUPLES
by Susan E. Johnson. 352 pp. Joys of coupledom.
ISBN 0-941-483-75-4   12.95

SLICK by Camarin Grae. 304 pp. Exotic, erotic adventure.
ISBN 0-941483-74-6   9.95

NINTH LIFE by Lauren Wright Douglas. 256 pp. A Caitlin
Reece mystery. 2nd in a series.   ISBN 0-941483-50-9   8.95

PLAYERS by Robbi Sommers. 192 pp. Sizzling, erotic novel.
ISBN 0-941483-73-8   8.95

MURDER AT RED ROOK RANCH by Dorothy Tell. 224 pp.
First Poppy Dillworth adventure.   ISBN 0-941483-80-0   8.95

LESBIAN SURVIVAL MANUAL by Rhonda Dicksion.
112 pp. Cartoons!   ISBN 0-941483-71-1   8.95

A ROOM FULL OF WOMEN by Elisabeth Nonas. 256 pp.
Contemporary Lesbian lives.   ISBN 0-941483-69-X   8.95

MURDER IS RELATIVE by Karen Saum. 256 pp. The first
Brigid Donovan mystery.   ISBN 0-941483-70-3   8.95
PRIORITIES by Lynda Lyons 288 pp. Science fiction with
a twist.   ISBN 0-941483-66-5   8.95
THEME FOR DIVERSE INSTRUMENTS by Jane Rule. 208
pp. Powerful romantic lesbian stories. ISBN 0-941483-63-0   8.95
LESBIAN QUERIES by Hertz & Ertman. 112 pp. The questions
you were too embarrassed to ask.   ISBN 0-941483-67-3   8.95
CLUB 12 by Amanda Kyle Williams. 288 pp. Espionage thriller
featuring a lesbian agent!   ISBN 0-941483-64-9   8.95
DEATH DOWN UNDER by Claire McNab. 240 pp. 3rd Det.
Insp. Carol Ashton mystery.   ISBN 0-941483-39-8   8.95
MONTANA FEATHERS by Penny Hayes. 256 pp. Vivian and
Elizabeth find love in frontier Montana. ISBN 0-941483-61-4 8.95
CHESAPEAKE PROJECT by Phyllis Horn. 304 pp. Jessie &
Meredith in perilous adventure.   ISBN 0-941483-58-4   8.95
LIFESTYLES by Jackie Calhoun. 224 pp. Contemporary Lesbian
lives and loves.   ISBN 0-941483-57-6   8.95
VIRAGO by Karen Marie Christa Minns. 208 pp. Darsen has
chosen Ginny.   ISBN 0-941483-56-8   8.95
WILDERNESS TREK by Dorothy Tell. 192 pp. Six women on
vacation learning "new" skills.   ISBN 0-941483-60-6   8.95
MURDER BY THE BOOK by Pat Welch. 256 pp. A Helen
Black Mystery. First in a series.   ISBN 0-941483-59-2   8.95
BERRIGAN by Vicki P. McConnell. 176 pp. Youthful Lesbian-
romantic, idealistic Berrigan.   ISBN 0-941483-55-X   8.95
LESBIANS IN GERMANY by Lillian Faderman & B. Eriksson.
128 pp. Fiction, poetry, essays.   ISBN 0-941483-62-2   8.95
THE BEVERLY MALIBU by Katherine V. Forrest. 288 pp. A
Kate Delafield Mystery. 3rd in a series. ISBN 0-941483-47-9 16.95
THERE'S SOMETHING I'VE BEEN MEANING TO TELL
YOU Ed. by Loralee MacPike. 288 pp. Gay men and lesbians
coming out to their children.   ISBN 0-941483-44-4   9.95
                                       ISBN 0-941483-54-1   16.95
LIFTING BELLY by Gertrude Stein. Ed. by Rebecca Mark. 104
pp. Erotic poetry.   ISBN 0-941483-51-7   8.95
                                       ISBN 0-941483-53-3   14.95
ROSE PENSKI by Roz Perry. 192 pp. Adult lovers in a long-term
relationship.   ISBN 0-941483-37-1   8.95
AFTER THE FIRE by Jane Rule. 256 pp. Warm, human novel
by this incomparable author.   ISBN 0-941483-45-2   8.95

SUE SLATE, PRIVATE EYE by Lee Lynch. 176 pp. The gay
folk of Peacock Alley are *all* cats.   ISBN 0-941483-52-5   8.95

CHRIS by Randy Salem. 224 pp. Golden oldie. Handsome Chris
and her adventures.   ISBN 0-941483-42-8   8.95

THREE WOMEN by March Hastings. 232 pp. Golden oldie. A
triangle among wealthy sophisticates.   ISBN 0-941483-43-6   8.95

RICE AND BEANS by Valeria Taylor. 232 pp. Love and
romance on poverty row.   ISBN 0-941483-41-X   8.95

PLEASURES by Robbi Sommers. 204 pp. Unprecedented
eroticism.   ISBN 0-941483-49-5   8.95

EDGEWISE by Camarin Grae. 372 pp. Spellbinding
adventure.   ISBN 0-941483-19-3   9.95

FATAL REUNION by Claire McNab. 216 pp. 2nd Det. Inspec.
Carol Ashton mystery.   ISBN 0-941483-40-1   8.95

KEEP TO ME STRANGER by Sarah Aldridge. 372 pp. Romance
set in a department store dynasty.   ISBN 0-941483-38-X   9.95

HEARTSCAPE by Sue Gambill. 204 pp. American lesbian in
Portugal.   ISBN 0-941483-33-9   8.95

IN THE BLOOD by Lauren Wright Douglas. 252 pp. Lesbian
science fiction adventure fantasy   ISBN 0-941483-22-3   8.95

THE BEE'S KISS by Shirley Verel. 216 pp. Delicate, delicious
romance.   ISBN 0-941483-36-3   8.95

RAGING MOTHER MOUNTAIN by Pat Emmerson. 264 pp.
Furosa Firechild's adventures in Wonderland.   ISBN 0-941483-35-5   8.95

IN EVERY PORT by Karin Kallmaker. 228 pp. Jessica's sexy,
adventuresome travels.   ISBN 0-941483-37-7   8.95

OF LOVE AND GLORY by Evelyn Kennedy. 192 pp. Exciting
WWII romance.   ISBN 0-941483-32-0   8.95

CLICKING STONES by Nancy Tyler Glenn. 288 pp. Love
transcending time.   ISBN 0-941483-31-2   8.95

SURVIVING SISTERS by Gail Pass. 252 pp. Powerful love
story.   ISBN 0-941483-16-9   8.95

SOUTH OF THE LINE by Catherine Ennis. 216 pp. Civil War
adventure.   ISBN 0-941483-29-0   8.95

WOMAN PLUS WOMAN by Dolores Klaich. 300 pp. Supurb
Lesbian overview.   ISBN 0-941483-28-2   9.95

SLOW DANCING AT MISS POLLY'S by Sheila Ortiz Taylor.
96 pp. Lesbian Poetry   ISBN 0-941483-30-4   7.95

DOUBLE DAUGHTER by Vicki P. McConnell. 216 pp. A Nyla
Wade Mystery, third in the series.   ISBN 0-941483-26-6   8.95

HEAVY GILT by Delores Klaich. 192 pp. Lesbian detective/
disappearing homophobes/upper class gay society.
ISBN 0-941483-25-8   8.95

THE FINER GRAIN by Denise Ohio. 216 pp. Brilliant young
college lesbian novel.   ISBN 0-941483-11-8   8.95

THE AMAZON TRAIL by Lee Lynch. 216 pp. Life, travel & lore
of famous lesbian author.   ISBN 0-941483-27-4   8.95

HIGH CONTRAST by Jessie Lattimore. 264 pp. Women of the
Crystal Palace.   ISBN 0-941483-17-7   8.95

OCTOBER OBSESSION by Meredith More. Josie's rich, secret
Lesbian life.   ISBN 0-941483-18-5   8.95

LESBIAN CROSSROADS by Ruth Baetz. 276 pp. Contemporary
Lesbian lives.   ISBN 0-941483-21-5   9.95

BEFORE STONEWALL: THE MAKING OF A GAY AND
LESBIAN COMMUNITY by Andrea Weiss & Greta Schiller.
96 pp., 25 illus.   ISBN 0-941483-20-7   7.95

WE WALK THE BACK OF THE TIGER by Patricia A. Murphy.
192 pp. Romantic Lesbian novel/beginning women's movement.
ISBN 0-941483-13-4   8.95

SUNDAY'S CHILD by Joyce Bright. 216 pp. Lesbian athletics, at
last the novel about sports.   ISBN 0-941483-12-6   8.95

OSTEN'S BAY by Zenobia N. Vole. 204 pp. Sizzling adventure
romance set on Bonaire.   ISBN 0-941483-15-0   8.95

LESSONS IN MURDER by Claire McNab. 216 pp. 1st Det. Inspec.
Carol Ashton mystery — erotic tension!. ISBN 0-941483-14-2   8.95

YELLOWTHROAT by Penny Hayes. 240 pp. Margarita, bandit,
kidnaps Julia.   ISBN 0-941483-10-X   8.95

SAPPHISTRY: THE BOOK OF LESBIAN SEXUALITY by
Pat Califia. 3d edition, revised. 208 pp.   ISBN 0-941483-24-X   8.95

CHERISHED LOVE by Evelyn Kennedy. 192 pp. Erotic
Lesbian love story.   ISBN 0-941483-08-8   8.95

LAST SEPTEMBER by Helen R. Hull. 208 pp. Six stories & a
glorious novella.   ISBN 0-941483-09-6   8.95

THE SECRET IN THE BIRD by Camarin Grae. 312 pp. Striking,
psychological suspense novel.   ISBN 0-941483-05-3   8.95

TO THE LIGHTNING by Catherine Ennis. 208 pp. Romantic
Lesbian 'Robinson Crusoe' adventure.   ISBN 0-941483-06-1   8.95

THE OTHER SIDE OF VENUS by Shirley Verel. 224 pp.
Luminous, romantic love story.   ISBN 0-941483-07-X   8.95

DREAMS AND SWORDS by Katherine V. Forrest. 192 pp.
Romantic, erotic, imaginative stories.   ISBN 0-941483-03-7   8.95

MEMORY BOARD by Jane Rule. 336 pp. Memorable novel
about an aging Lesbian couple.   ISBN 0-941483-02-9   9.95

THE ALWAYS ANONYMOUS BEAST by Lauren Wright
Douglas. 224 pp. A Caitlin Reece mystery. First in a series.
    ISBN 0-941483-04-5   8.95

SEARCHING FOR SPRING by Patricia A. Murphy. 224 pp.
Novel about the recovery of love.   ISBN 0-941483-00-2   8.95

DUSTY'S QUEEN OF HEARTS DINER by Lee Lynch. 240 pp.
Romantic blue-collar novel.   ISBN 0-941483-01-0   8.95

PARENTS MATTER by Ann Muller. 240 pp. Parents'
relationships with Lesbian daughters and gay sons.
    ISBN 0-930044-91-6   9.95

THE PEARLS by Shelley Smith. 176 pp. Passion and fun in
the Caribbean sun.   ISBN 0-930044-93-2   7.95

MAGDALENA by Sarah Aldridge. 352 pp. Epic Lesbian novel
set on three continents.   ISBN 0-930044-99-1   8.95

THE BLACK AND WHITE OF IT by Ann Allen Shockley.
144 pp. Short stories.   ISBN 0-930044-96-7   7.95

SAY JESUS AND COME TO ME by Ann Allen Shockley. 288
pp. Contemporary romance.   ISBN 0-930044-98-3   8.95

LOVING HER by Ann Allen Shockley. 192 pp. Romantic love
story.   ISBN 0-930044-97-5   7.95

MURDER AT THE NIGHTWOOD BAR by Katherine V.
Forrest. 240 pp. A Kate Delafield mystery. Second in a series.
    ISBN 0-930044-92-4   8.95

ZOE'S BOOK by Gail Pass. 224 pp. Passionate, obsessive love
story.   ISBN 0-930044-95-9   7.95

WINGED DANCER by Camarin Grae. 228 pp. Erotic Lesbian
adventure story.   ISBN 0-930044-88-6   9.95

PAZ by Camarin Grae. 336 pp. Romantic Lesbian adventurer
with the power to change the world.   ISBN 0-930044-89-4   8.95

SOUL SNATCHER by Camarin Grae. 224 pp. A puzzle, an
adventure, a mystery -- Lesbian romance.   ISBN 0-930044-90-8   8.95

THE LOVE OF GOOD WOMEN by Isabel Miller. 224 pp.
Long-awaited new novel by the author of the beloved *Patience
and Sarah.*   ISBN 0-930044-81-9   8.95

THE HOUSE AT PELHAM FALLS by Brenda Weathers. 240
pp. Suspenseful Lesbian ghost story.   ISBN 0-930044-79-7   7.95

HOME IN YOUR HANDS by Lee Lynch. 240 pp. More stories
from the author of *Old Dyke Tales.*   ISBN 0-930044-80-0   7.95

EACH HAND A MAP by Anita Skeen. 112 pp. Real-life poems
that touch us all.   ISBN 0-930044-82-7   6.95

SURPLUS by Sylvia Stevenson. 342 pp. A classic early Lesbian
novel. ISBN 0-930044-78-9 7.95

PEMBROKE PARK by Michelle Martin. 256 pp. Derring-do
and daring romance in Regency England. ISBN 0-930044-77-0 7.95

THE LONG TRAIL by Penny Hayes. 248 pp. Vivid adventures
of two women in love in the old west. ISBN 0-930044-76-2 8.95

HORIZON OF THE HEART by Shelley Smith. 192 pp. Hot
romance in summertime New England. ISBN 0-930044-75-4 7.95

AN EMERGENCE OF GREEN by Katherine V. Forrest. 288
pp. Powerful novel of sexual discovery. ISBN 0-930044-69-X 8.95

THE LESBIAN PERIODICALS INDEX edited by Claire
Potter. 432 pp. Author & subject index. ISBN 0-930044-74-6 29.95

DESERT OF THE HEART by Jane Rule. 224 pp. A classic;
basis for the movie *Desert Hearts*. ISBN 0-930044-73-8 8.95

SPRING FORWARD/FALL BACK by Sheila Ortiz Taylor.
288 pp. Literary novel of timeless love. ISBN 0-930044-70-3 7.95

FOR KEEPS by Elisabeth Nonas. 144 pp. Contemporary novel
about losing and finding love. ISBN 0-930044-71-1 7.95

TORCHLIGHT TO VALHALLA by Gale Wilhelm. 128 pp.
Classic novel by a great Lesbian writer. ISBN 0-930044-68-1 7.95

LESBIAN NUNS: BREAKING SILENCE edited by Rosemary
Curb and Nancy Manahan. 432 pp. Unprecedented autobiographies
of religious life. ISBN 0-930044-62-2 9.95

THE SWASHBUCKLER by Lee Lynch. 288 pp. Colorful novel
set in Greenwich Village in the sixties. ISBN 0-930044-66-5 8.95

MISFORTUNE'S FRIEND by Sarah Aldridge. 320 pp. Historical Lesbian novel set on two continents. ISBN 0-930044-67-3 7.95

A STUDIO OF ONE'S OWN by Ann Stokes. Edited by
Dolores Klaich. 128 pp. Autobiography. ISBN 0-930044-64-9 7.95

SEX VARIANT WOMEN IN LITERATURE by Jeannette
Howard Foster. 448 pp. Literary history. ISBN 0-930044-65-7 8.95

A HOT-EYED MODERATE by Jane Rule. 252 pp. Hard-hitting
essays on gay life; writing; art. ISBN 0-930044-57-6 7.95

INLAND PASSAGE AND OTHER STORIES by Jane Rule.
288 pp. Wide-ranging new collection. ISBN 0-930044-56-8 7.95

WE TOO ARE DRIFTING by Gale Wilhelm. 128 pp. Timeless
Lesbian novel, a masterpiece. ISBN 0-930044-61-4 6.95

AMATEUR CITY by Katherine V. Forrest. 224 pp. A Kate
Delafield mystery. First in a series. ISBN 0-930044-55-X 8.95

THE SOPHIE HOROWITZ STORY by Sarah Schulman. 176
pp. Engaging novel of madcap intrigue. ISBN 0-930044-54-1 7.95

THE BURNTON WIDOWS by Vickie P. McConnell. 272 pp. A
Nyla Wade mystery, second in the series. ISBN 0-930044-52-5   7.95

OLD DYKE TALES by Lee Lynch. 224 pp. Extraordinary
stories of our diverse Lesbian lives. ISBN 0-930044-51-7   8.95

DAUGHTERS OF A CORAL DAWN by Katherine V. Forrest.
240 pp. Novel set in a Lesbian new world. ISBN 0-930044-50-9   8.95

AGAINST THE SEASON by Jane Rule. 224 pp. Luminous,
complex novel of interrelationships. ISBN 0-930044-48-7   8.95

LOVERS IN THE PRESENT AFTERNOON by Kathleen
Fleming. 288 pp. A novel about recovery and growth.
ISBN 0-930044-46-0   8.95

TOOTHPICK HOUSE by Lee Lynch. 264 pp. Love between
two Lesbians of different classes. ISBN 0-930044-45-2   7.95

MADAME AURORA by Sarah Aldridge. 256 pp. Historical
novel featuring a charismatic "seer." ISBN 0-930044-44-4   7.95

CURIOUS WINE by Katherine V. Forrest. 176 pp. Passionate
Lesbian love story, a best-seller. ISBN 0-930044-43-6   8.95

BLACK LESBIAN IN WHITE AMERICA by Anita Cornwell.
141 pp. Stories, essays, autobiography. ISBN 0-930044-41-X   7.95

CONTRACT WITH THE WORLD by Jane Rule. 340 pp.
Powerful, panoramic novel of gay life. ISBN 0-930044-28-2   9.95

MRS. PORTER'S LETTER by Vicki P. McConnell. 224 pp.
The first Nyla Wade mystery. ISBN 0-930044-29-0   7.95

TO THE CLEVELAND STATION by Carol Anne Douglas.
192 pp. Interracial Lesbian love story. ISBN 0-930044-27-4   6.95

THE NESTING PLACE by Sarah Aldridge. 224 pp. A
three-woman triangle--love conquers all! ISBN 0-930044-26-6   7.95

THIS IS NOT FOR YOU by Jane Rule. 284 pp. A letter to a
beloved is also an intricate novel. ISBN 0-930044-25-8   8.95

FAULTLINE by Sheila Ortiz Taylor. 140 pp. Warm, funny,
literate story of a startling family. ISBN 0-930044-24-X   6.95

THE LESBIAN IN LITERATURE by Barbara Grier. 3d ed.
Foreword by Maida Tilchen. 240 pp. Comprehensive bibliography.
Literary ratings; rare photos. ISBN 0-930044-23-1   7.95

ANNA'S COUNTRY by Elizabeth Lang. 208 pp. A woman
finds her Lesbian identity. ISBN 0-930044-19-3   8.95

PRISM by Valerie Taylor. 158 pp. A love affair between two
women in their sixties. ISBN 0-930044-18-5   6.95

BLACK LESBIANS: AN ANNOTATED BIBLIOGRAPHY
compiled by J. R. Roberts. Foreword by Barbara Smith. 112 pp.
Award-winning bibliography. ISBN 0-930044-21-5   5.95

THE MARQUISE AND THE NOVICE by Victoria Ramstetter.
108 pp. A Lesbian Gothic novel.   ISBN 0-930044-16-9   6.95

OUTLANDER by Jane Rule. 207 pp. Short stories and essays
by one of our finest writers.   ISBN 0-930044-17-7   8.95

ALL TRUE LOVERS by Sarah Aldridge. 292 pp. Romantic
novel set in the 1930s and 1940s.   ISBN 0-930044-10-X   8.95

A WOMAN APPEARED TO ME by Renee Vivien. 65 pp. A
classic; translated by Jeannette H. Foster. ISBN 0-930044-06-1   5.00

CYTHEREA'S BREATH by Sarah Aldridge. 240 pp. Romantic
novel about women's entrance into medicine.
                                             ISBN 0-930044-02-9   6.95

TOTTIE by Sarah Aldridge. 181 pp. Lesbian romance in the
turmoil of the sixties.   ISBN 0-930044-01-0   6.95

THE LATECOMER by Sarah Aldridge. 107 pp. A delicate love
story.   ISBN 0-930044-00-2   6.95

ODD GIRL OUT by Ann Bannon.   ISBN 0-930044-83-5   5.95

I AM A WOMAN by Ann Bannon.   ISBN 0-930044-84-3   5.95

WOMEN IN THE SHADOWS by Ann Bannon.
                                             ISBN 0-930044-85-1   5.95

JOURNEY TO A WOMAN by Ann Bannon.
                                             ISBN 0-930044-86-X   5.95

BEEBO BRINKER by Ann Bannon.   ISBN 0-930044-87-8   5.95
          Legendary novels written in the fifties and sixties,
               set in the gay mecca of Greenwich Village.

VOLUTE BOOKS

JOURNEY TO FULFILLMENT   Early classics by Valerie   3.95

A WORLD WITHOUT MEN   Taylor: The Erika Frohmann   3.95

RETURN TO LESBOS   series.   3.95

These are just a few of the many Naiad Press titles — we are the oldest and
largest lesbian/feminist publishing company in the world. Please request a
complete catalog. We offer personal service; we encourage and welcome direct
mail orders from individuals who have limited access to bookstores carrying
our publications.